WAGGING TALES
VOLUME 2

The Last Cheetah

and other stories

Vijay Padaki

notionpress.com

INDIA · SINGAPORE · MALAYSIA

For

Shabari

“*Vijay's stories don't so much transport me to another world as take me to other planes of this one. They are a hall of mirrors where each reflection gives us a glimpse of the extraordinary in what seems at first to be a mundane life. His tales never fail to remind me that everyone is unique, complex, born from miraculous histories, carriers of the oldest tragedies and most ancient mythologies, without even realizing it.*

Jeffrey Stanley
Fulbright Ambassador, Playwright,
Professor of Stage and Film writing, Drexel University and Tisch School

Vijay Padaki's stories are arresting for his range of subjects, not restricted by class, religion or ethnicity. They are those of an observer who has had a multitude of experiences but who has kept a wry distance from the human situations that have excited his imagination. Although he has evident sympathies he does not take sides or judge, and his concise prose delivers each tale with an impact that should be the envy of most Indian fiction writers in English today.”

MK Raghavendra
Cultural, Film and Literary critic and Writer

Vijay's stories, like his plays, have a cinematic quality to them. The imagery makes available lasting images that forge their way through profound and deceptive simplicity of woven words. The punch moves subtly, almost imperceptibly, through the fabric of language to make for the unexpected twist at the end, time and again, as always.

Padmavati Rao
Actor, Poet, Storyteller, Educator

These short stories will bring you the old world fragrance of fresh coffee in a tumbler and firewood in the old bath house. Vijay Padaki melds his background in psychology, theatre and management to bring alive characters, relationships, dynamics and interactions in unique settings. The detailing and denouement in each story is exquisite.

Shekhar Seshadri
Child & Adolescent Psychiatrist,
Theatre Educator, Musician

ISBN 979-8-89588-659-5

CONTENTS

Telling Stories

A few ideas have stayed with me over many years. The first is that when the human animal discovered the advantages of living and moving in groups, rather than as loner hunter-gatherers, the first joy was in the new experience of sharing – sharing food from the hunt, sharing experiences from the hunt, sharing learnings, sharing ideas...sharing stories. The craft of storytelling was recognized for its value as early as the craft of making spears or skinning animals.

The second idea is something I picked up from an old British playwright friend who, unfortunately, is no more. It was a most remarkable idea. He said that mankind has only six stories. The six stories are based on a small number of primal experiences for which the human species has an innate capacity. All the stories ever told by mankind are really combinations of these primal experiences. The combinations can be infinite, of course. Not very different from the infinite range of hues that a paint company can turn out for us – all from three basic colours. The same as the three concentrates in your colour printer.

The third is that all writing is autobiographical. The qualifier would be: to greater or lesser extent. What that means is that life experiences have a way of creeping into everything we say. In other words, there is no need to deny it or be sorry about it. I have had the good fortune of exposures in life that had both breadth and depth. These included field experiences as part of work in large development programmes in rural settings. There is also the curse of indelible memory one has learned to live with. Ah, that is a story in itself. Not surprisingly, many of my stories (not all) are 'case studies', but retold in fictional form.

The fourth is a human characteristic that is usually not given sufficient attention. It is undoubtedly the most fascinating characteristic of the human animal. Among all the 8.7 million species of life on this earth, it is only the human animal that inflicts its experiences on fellow humans. It is the only species that has storytellers. And invents infinite varieties of construction to tell the same six stories.

So...Here I am, trying to hold your attention with a bunch of stories that I have the audacity to believe are original! Here is a paragraph I wrote once to serve as an over-riding preface to every story in my collection of plays for the stage and, now, short stories for reading.

> *I shall cut a long story short. It is a tale that is very old, as old as mankind itself. It has been engraved on stone tablets, inscribed on palm leaves, inked by hand on stretches of hand-made papyrus and passed on in oral storytelling traditions wherever communities gathered to assert their belongingness. It is a tale that can be told through the night or printed on hundreds of pages. I have chosen to tell you the tale in ten minutes. Don't go away if you are listening to me. Don't put the pages down if you are reading. Surely you can spare ten minutes to know what I wish to share with you.*

A final thought. I have had the good fortune to be invited to read my stories to small invited audiences. I discovered first hand then what wise writers have known all along – that the heard text can give us new meanings that the read text does not. I soon found myself writing stories for reading out. It came easily, I suppose, because of the past writing for the stage. The readings have often helped me refine the text. I would like to imagine the stories in this collection having many more readings, even rendered as storytelling theatre.

Many thanks to the close circle that endured the first drafts of these stories. Their comments were always valuable. The circle included Vijji Chari, Madhu Shukla, Priya Rao, Minti Jain, Naveen Tater, Murtuza Khetty, Malavika Kapur and Sudhir and Asha Vombatkere. A second group, comprising the family circle of Chatura, Shabari, Rupande and Shiv, were conscripted into detention for some first readings. More recently Kumkum Amin, taking to writing herself, commented on a few stories. Padmavati (Pinty) Rao and I have done readings together. She convinced me ever so gently that the stories should be published.

I could think of nobody else but Deepak Mote to take charge of the formidable tasks of design, layout and supervision of the publication process.

Vijay Padaki

The Kiss

It was time to go. They kissed. It was not what it used to be, but it was not cursory. It was not insincere. Neither could help thinking about it. It was not passionate. It did not lack feeling. They kissed. It was not insincere. It was different. Their feelings stood suspended, still warm, still recognizable as feelings, but their thoughts were about their thoughts at the moment, racing left and right between the newness of this kiss and the thought that this would be their last kiss. Neither knew what was correct for the occasion. How light or hard should the lips press? How much should they part? How long should it be held? What to do with the hands? Both knew that they were both struggling as hard with the same questions of what to say and what to do. And what not to do. They moved apart at the same moment. They smiled. They knew instantly that there was no need to find some clever description of the moment, and no need to say it. They smiled again. It was not insincere.

Rahul first met Radha at the college tea shop. Within a month they were permanent fixtures at the cafeteria. The same table, the same seats at the table, the same hours of the day. Later, when other pieces of furniture in other locations demanded more of their presence, they still found time to return to the corner table at the cafeteria in an act of reverence. They were called Rara on campus by their friends. Ah, but everybody in the world seemed to know Rara. A friend of theirs once hailed an auto rickshaw to get to the mall, and the driver said he had already been booked by Rara. The owner of the tuck shop at the college gate had a page in his account book with the name Rara.

How strange that she was now going to marry a man called Rakesh. What would the two of them be called in the new circle of friends that took them in? Rahul tried to fight off the thought, but he realized at the same moment that he was not really upset. Not disturbed, not angry. Perhaps a bit amused that he was struggling with a thought that was really harmless. He imagined a group of well dressed men and women meeting on a Friday evening at a fashionable club, and one of them looking around and saying "Where's Rara? What's keeping them?" Exactly the way Chika and Duggu and others in the gang said it now. Till the other day. He smiled when he thought of that. She smiled too. He wondered what she had on her mind.

"You know what I am thinking" she asked. Rahul nodded as if to say yes and no. "I am thinking what a lucky girl I have been all my life so far. So lucky and so happy. And you... have been so much a part of that happiness..."

But... thought Rahul. We must get on, mustn't we? Please, Radha, he thought again, let us not destroy this beautiful moment with petty doggerel. But he simply nodded some more.

"You know what?" she asked, after the longest pause, held with the longest smile. "I don't think we should destroy this beautiful moment with petty doggerel."

And then, "You will come to the reception, won't you? The whole gang will be there. I will look out for you."

She turned and darted off. Was this the end of the meeting Rahul had prepared himself for? No, she stopped at the stairway and added, "Oh, you can come to the wedding too, of course, but you know you will be bored to death by the ceremony. Or choked to death before that." It was not insincere. She was off. The end.

⁂

No, he would not go to the wedding. Yes, he would go to the reception. Yes, he went to the wedding. The gang insisted, and he went along. They decided to meet outside the wedding hall, at the florist across the street, and go in all together. They stuck together through the morning and through lunch, and even left the hall together. They made sure Rahul was well protected, forming a ring around him at times. It must all have been planned in secret the day before. Rahul thought there was a drop in the noise level inside the hall when the gang made its appearance. They were looking at him. Every now and then he saw people in twos and threes putting their heads together and then one of them looking in his direction. Somebody in the gang would take a step gently and block the view. Of course he knew what they were saying, what they were thinking. He was brave, wasn't he? Such a sport, isn't he? Most inauspicious, his being here, isn't it? He is available now, isn't he? He was the one, wasn't he?

Rahul realized he was tense. He had not slept well the previous night. There was a tingling sensation in his lower back that came in waves every ten minutes. Why was the gang standing through the ceremony? He wanted so much to sit. Seeing an empty chair on one side Rahul slipped out of the ring and slid onto the white plastic seat. The next moment the wave took over and he was in pain. He rose immediately, cautiously, concealing the pain. There were eyes turning to see him from every part of the hall. The gang moved quickly to greet the safari suited gentleman in the next chair and threw a ring around Rahul once again. One of them asked if he was in pain. Rahul smiled. It felt better, he said. It was true. He smiled and he felt better. Everybody noticed that, didn't they? He had such an after shave lotion smile. He looked so relaxed. Such a sport.

They came with the plate of rice grains. Time up. It would soon be over. Then lunch, and then close of play. The gang pushed the plate towards Rahul and he picked up his handful, smiling. He bent his head forward to look into the grains in his palm. His mind was racing. A tablespoon of rice in every palm. Five hundred palms. That would be about how many kilograms of rice? And that would be... A hand tapped his shoulder. It was one of the gang. He looked up to see a bridegroom on the stage holding a gold chain in front of him. What was his name? It started with Ra, did it not? Was it Rakesh? Yes, it was. Rakesh. He seemed to be saying he was ready to embark on some sort of conquest. Was that Radha next to him? Yes, it was. She had her head bent, as if to say go ahead, chop it off.

The hand that tapped his shoulder now rested there, a light, assuring grip, as if to say that watching a community animal sacrifice is part of growing up. He turned to Rahul and smiled. Ah, yes, the smile. It was a momentary lapse. Rahul smiled again and the video game playing before him vanished. Radha turned to the gathering in the hall one last time. She seemed frightened. No, she was calm. Was she calmly resigned? Calmly stoic? Just before she turned back she caught a glimpse of Rahul. Did she? She must have. Was that a smile? Yes, it was. Was she...? A senior looking member of Radha's family had now stepped in front of her, raising both his arms and signaling frantically to the musicians at the entrance of the hall. They responded instantly and threw in the orgasmic crescendo of drum beats and shrieking pipes. Rahul and the gang threw in the rice. The deed was done. Throwing the rice felt good. Rahul had managed to step out of the ring towards the stage to throw the rice. He was not stopped. He threw the rice at the sacrifice. It felt good.

The gang decided to offer greetings and gifts immediately after, before the line got too long. They were up on the stage within minutes. Radha saw them approaching and nudged her newly acquired dhoti clad conqueror, preparing him. Ah, that smile. She was whispering something to him. What was she saying about Rahul? What would she say later, at night, after her head was chopped off in ecstasy? What would he say in return?

"Ah, you must be Rahul! Radha has been..." The line was cut off. Radha was introducing him to the others. The huddle was quickly straightened out for the cameras. With the sun lamp blazing before them he heard her plead, "Once more before you go?"

Rakesh added, "Once more, you must all have lunch before you go." The group left the stage in single file and headed straight away to the lunch service in the basement hall. Placing himself at the tail end of the line Rahul tried to get one last glimpse of her on the way out. She wasn't looking.

⁂ ⁂ ⁂ ⁂ ⁂

Rahul slept surprisingly well that night. He felt a lightness when he went to bed. He felt brighter when he awoke the next morning. As he sniffed the coffee and took the first sips he thought it was not surprising after all. The act of tossing the rice had somehow changed him. He had turned into a well-wisher and even a champion of the new alliance. He felt himself turning into – what was the word – a protector. It felt good. Being a protector felt good. It was not clear yet what he was protecting. Or why. It was only clear that this very important responsibility had now been placed on his shoulders. The job description would be spelt out in due course. He couldn't wait to meet the gang and tell them about it. It would be at the reception that evening.

On second thoughts, he decided to wait a while before sharing his revelation with them. They might not understand. They might misunderstand. Worse, they might... No, there was no hurry to bring them into this. Besides, he might not even go to the reception in the evening. The more important presence at the wedding had already been accomplished. Nobody would be missed at the reception.

Very quickly the plan for the evening fell into place. A bottle of red, some fine pasta, a walnut-crust pie and lots of Beethoven. In fact he would spend the morning spring cleaning his one-roomer and prettying up the place. He had to admit it was mess. He hadn't realized how much neglect he had slipped into in the last few months. He would begin with the stacks of old magazines under the bed and the pile of unwashed linen next to the shoe rack. Should he have somebody join him in the evening? Nah! They would all be going to the reception anyway. Maybe Rita, who was part of the gang and yet not part of it? He walked up to the phone, picked up the receiver and.... Nah, what would she think, being asked about Beethoven's Seventh while her mind was at the reception? Another time, perhaps. He walked back to the coffee table. The phone rang.

"Hi! How are you this morning?" It was Rita.

"Well..."

"Hi! Are you there? Can you hear me? I can call later if you like."

"No, no... I was just... It was telepathy, I think. Hi, good morning."

"Good morning. Were you thinking of me?"

"Yes... no, not you, really, the gang... I was thinking of all of you."

"Really! What were you thinking?"

"I was wondering about the reception this evening. You see, I was..."

"Well, that's what I am calling you about. The gang asked me to find out what you'd think about skipping the reception and meeting up at your place."

"My place?"

"Yes, we could pot luck there. A pasta party maybe. We could just relax, listen to some good music, chat, just chill out a bit after the hectic week..."

"Sounds good."

"Super! I will tell them." Click.

Action stations! Rahul put the coffee mug away and began his attack on the magazines and the linen.

Rita was very understanding. It was an unspoken pact. She would not ask about his past. He would not ask about hers. She did have a past, didn't she? There was this executive type with a job in Bombay who was making week-end trips to see her. The gang knew about him, of course, but she kept him out of all conversations and all outings. They knew nothing about him. They were itching to know, but were awed by Rita's utter silence on the matter, and chose to let it stay that way. And now, here she was, more fully a part of the gang, her week-ends free.

She loved music, she said. Not Beethoven, but the other stuff in Rahul's room. She would switch on the system as soon as she entered. "What shall I play for you?" she would ask. She had rearranged all the CDs and all the cassettes, and knew exactly where to find what.

"What shall I play for you?"

"Oh, whatever you like."

It was the same every visit. Every Thursday evening, straight from her art appreciation class. It was now, what, three months since the first pasta party. And two months since the first time she showed she was taking charge. She didn't seem to care if it was Pink Floyd or Frank Zappa or Mendelssohn. She had to switch on the system on arrival. Was the music for Rahul or herself? Was it the music or was it the sound of his system that she wanted? Thursdays were getting to be fun. Rahul was discovering the joy of having music on while she was switching him on.

⌘ ⌘ ⌘ ⌘ ⌘

Surabhi was very understanding. It was an unspoken pact. She would not ask about his past. He would not ask about hers, which was well known in all parts of the world that mattered, a grand total of one man in her life, as it was in the beginning, was now, and would ever be, world without end. Amen. Panchu was his name, and he basked in the glory of her devotion.

She loved to cook, she said. She loved to cook for Rahul. Tuesday dinners were Surabhi specials. She would come over directly from the dance studio, a string bag with a change of clothes in one hand and a Tupperware dabba of masalas and toppings in the other. Panchu sent his love.

"Panchu says Hi!" The first words Rahul would hear every time he opened the door, every Tuesday.

"Uh huh. And what does the chef recommend today?"

"Oh, it is a Tuesday surprise! A mandatory wink, and she would go directly into the kitchen. It had changed a bit a month ago. A mandatory hug and off to the kitchen. Moments later it was off to the bathroom for a quick shower and change, and then it was Tuesday evening once again.

The first time Surabhi brought a change in her bag she also brought back Rahul's lungi and kurta, taken the previous Tuesday, now laundered and ironed. She had come from the studio in her track suit was sweaty, and not very pleasant dinner company in that state, she said. Rahul's offer of a humble lungi and kurta was promptly accepted.

Rahul did notice that there was no talk of Panchu in recent times. And the hugs were just a little longer, a little closer. She stayed back longer too.

⌘ ⌘ ⌘ ⌘ ⌘

Arati on Mondays with her therapeutic yoga tips, Surabhi specials on Tuesdays, Vidya on Wednesdays with her twin Dalmatians, Rita on Thursdays for music lessons... Fridays, thank god, he had the evening to himself. Saturdays were still reserved for the gang, although they were not meeting as often. The number turning up was getting smaller. Where were the girls? It was getting too stag month by month. But they met anyway. And Sundays were for the family and housekeeping. Rahul lived a neater, cleaner life now. They called it a fuller life.

The best thing about the week was that it built up to the Friday just as Rahul wanted it. There was enough good food in the house, enough good wine, and he could listen to Beethoven as he ought to be heard. The girls would never understand. He never expected them to understand. They knew not what they knew not, and Rahul respected them for that. He took what they gave him, and they loved him for that. It was woven into the unspoken pact.

This Friday Rahul was determined to return to Beethoven's Seventh and to find out more about the sense of joy in the notes, the second movement widely regarded as maverick, the celebration of victory in a war of liberation. He would seek a fresh appreciation of the rhythmic structure, overpowering the melody. He would do this not by reading stale academic treatises, but by listening to the music in specially created conditions. The most important of these would be lying in the semi supine position Arati had taught him.

The preparations began soon after sunset. He lit the aromatic candles that need an hour to take effect. He adjusted the perforated brass lamp holder to throw its light patterns against the little bronze bust of Ludwig on the bookshelf. The curtains were changed to the peace inducing aqua green. The divan was cleared of all unnecessary cushions. Only a thin, flat fold of the handloom cover was kept at the head to aid the needed position recommended for relaxed concentration. He showered and shaved and changed into a lightly starched pure white cotton kurta-pyjama set. He practiced fifteen minutes of pranayama with the soft sound of the surf in the background. He was ready.

Serenely relaxed, Rahul stepped up to the music system and switched it on. Remote in hand, he took the prescribed position on the divan and switched on Beethoven's Seventh. The first movement opened. Rahul was completely prepared for this alap, the longest of Beethoven's introductions. Was it the longest in the history of the symphony? Hardly any melody at all, just a single note, a single pitch repeating itself. It was hypnotic, soothing, fascinating, a new meaning teasingly presented every few moments. Where was it heading? What next?

The doorbell! Six months ago Rahul would have cursed and ranted and even thrown a shoe at the door. Now he merely closed his eyes for a moment and rose calmly to switch on the main lights and turn down the music. He reached the door without yelling "Who is it?" or "Coming!" Who could it be at this hour on a Friday, he wondered. It was Radha.

Radha had the car and the driver. There was a furniture shop she had to go to less than a kilometer from Rahul's place. She decided to take a chance. Yes, she was shopping for furniture. They were furnishing the newly created annexe in her in-laws' bungalow. No, they did not move to a home of their own. Yes, she was settled in. And Rakesh? Oh, he was fine, promoted soon after the wedding, travelled a lot. No more. Topic change. What news of the gang? What was he busy with? What's new in music? And oh – his one-roomer was so cool! Rahul waited for the first burst to subside.

"It's been a while", he said softly. She fired again. "You've changed!"

"We all do, I suppose. We must, I suppose."

"I suppose so." Silence. Then, "I miss... the gang."

Rahul asked if he could arrange something. A good old pot luck maybe. Did she remember the last one?! When Chika and Duggu came in late and... "No", she cut in. "No, thanks. " Then, after a moment, "I am sorry... It won't work."

It was Rahul's turn to change the topic. It went from the new mall on the ring road to the reappearance of bicycles on roads to vermi-compost, the last link provided by Radha herself. "You know what", she asked, you could easily have a smart veggie garden right there in the balcony of this apartment."

Rahul said he would think about it. He was not insincere. She could easily drop in once a week and help him out, she said. She leaned across to say she was free on Fridays. There was great earnestness in her voice. Silence.

The Curse

It began when Sanjay opened his eyes. He had known that in the last few minutes before that he could not be sure if he was half awake or half asleep. The riddle lasted no longer than thirty minutes. Half asleep or half awake? In his room or somewhere else? Real or imagined? Is it happening to himself or is he watching it happening to him out there? Was the glass half empty or half full? The riddles in the last half hour before being on his feet were always delightful. He could say he looked forward to them. And then he would open his eyes. And close them again, forcing the enchanting state of limbo to hold just a wee bit longer.

It began when he opened his eyes. He was not asleep. The ceiling looked different. It was an empty expanse, dark and yet a visible expanse. When he turned to his left, which was the way he always got up, he saw a large stage with a wooden floor, bare. He saw that his bed was at the downstage end. It seemed to be on the stage and yet distanced from the stage. All around the bare floor, pushed to the edges, were pieces of the room furniture, strung like a garland. A tight spot came on slowly at the centre. It picked up a figure seated on the floor, bundled in a length of cloth, with only the face visible. The face was ashen, the eyes staring ahead. He saw that there were several layers of cloth bundling the person. It was not clear if the person was a man or a woman.

He knew where the light switch was and the way to the bathroom. But he remained in his bed, turned left, trying to see if it was somebody he knew. He then heard the sound of surf, gentle and peaceful. A group of six entered from several directions. He couldn't tell who they were or their ages. The sound gradually changed to a strong breeze, turning stormy. The group of six moved around the figure wrapped in cloth. The moves appeared to be practiced, but it was not a dance. One of them carefully removed a length of cloth, leaving other layers in place. More layers were removed by more members of the group. The layers seemed to be unending. The members of the group began playing and dancing with the lengths of cloth removed. They dropped the lengths of cloth on the floor, going on to remove more lengths. Finally, they left the lengths on the floor and started to leave the stage one by one. Two of them remained. They now appeared to be children. They surveyed the stage. They began placing the lengths of cloth back on the figure at the centre, one by one. The children left the stage after all the lengths of cloth were put back. The bare stage had only the figure at the centre once again, holding a large bundle, lengths of cloth. The sound subsided. It was still.

The figure rose, very slowly, stood still for a few moments, turned, and started to walk in a large circle, slowly. All the cloth was carried in front, in a bundle. The figure walked off stage with the bundle held close.

Slow fade out.

Sanjay knew it was time to roll over, put his feet into the slippers on the floor and get on his feet. He stepped to the left and flicked on the light switch. He tightened his eyelids in anticipation of the bright light above. The tube did not come on. There was a cone of purple light falling on the floor instead. It was from somewhere above, he could not tell from where, and it formed a spot in front of the bathroom door. Sanjay decided to get there anyway. As he stepped forward a shadow appeared from one side and stepped into the spot. It was the figure, without the bundle now. It beckoned Sanjay. As he reached the bathroom door the room got brighter. The figure placed a hand on Sanjay's shoulder and turned him around. It was his one-room apartment all right. The furniture was all in place. Everything was as it should be. The presence of the figure was the only thing out of place.

"Quite in place", said the figure. The words were spoken softly and clearly, in a tone that was probably a woman's. Sanjay turned to look into the figure's face. It was a man. The man pushed back the cloth covering his head and shoulders. He seemed a very old man. The wrinkles began where the silver hairline ended and spread all over his face, his neck, the shoulders and arms. He must have been at least a hundred years old. But he carried himself erect, his voice was very clear and it sounded young.

"No, I am not a hundred years old", he said. "It could be more than that. It could be less. I do not know exactly how old I am." Many questions rushed into Sanjay's head. But he was speechless. Even as he was struggling to find words to say something, the figure led him to a chair, seated him and continued.

"You want to know more." He pulled up another chair next to Sanjay, placed an arm on him, and continued. "I can tell you more. You look like a person who will listen. One who will understand. May I tell you more? You may nod to say yes."

Sanjay nodded. The figure then asked him to nod again if he would like a coffee. He would make two cups as Sanjay washed up in the bathroom. When he emerged, the figure was already seated, the two mugs of coffee on a stool before the two chairs. Sanjay sat next to the figure, picked up a mug and sipped his coffee, one little sip at a time, keeping his eyes on the figure all the time. "You want to know more", said the figure and sipped his own coffee, looking into the mug, not looking for a moment at Sanjay. When they were both done, the figure placed his empty mug on the stool, looked into Sanjay's eyes, smiled softly and said that he would be willing to tell Sanjay everything, in every detail, but on one condition. He should not be asked his name. And he should not be asked his age. It was part of the curse he was carrying. Sanjay asked if that was one condition or two. "Clever boy", the figure replied. No matter, he had no way to answer the two questions. Could he continue? Sanjay nodded to say yes.

⁂ ⁂ ⁂ ⁂ ⁂

"Chief Information Officer. That's what they call me. That's what I am at the Company. That's what I am in the community. Chief Information Officer." He said he belonged to a Brahmin agricultural family. They owned land, but did not cultivate it themselves. There were wage earning farmers who did that. He could not remember how many generations the family had lived in that village. The figure was one of four children born there. Sanjay asked how many years ago that was. The figure wagged a finger left and right to remind him that the question was not allowed. All he could say was that he could not tell. He had moved to the city to live with relatives while he studied in high school and college. He returned to the village home twice a year in the vacation breaks. He got a job soon after graduation. It was not difficult for a good student to get a good job in those days. The visits to the village continued, but they were shorter.

He took a deep breath and a long pause. He closed his eyes. It signaled his preparation for something important to follow. Sanjay understood. He waited patiently. When the figure opened his eyes, he looked up to ask silently if he should continue. Sanjay nodded yes. The story that followed is best reported in the figure's own words.

Sanjay had never ever attended to a person as closely as he did now. He recorded every word, every inflexion and every turn of phrase in his head. He found all his senses converging and tuned to the task. It was recorded as spoken by the figure, in the first person.

⌘ ⌘ ⌘ ⌘ ⌘

In one such visit I decided to go on a trek beyond the hills known as Devibetta. There was a shrine of Durgadevi on the other side, at the edge of a forest. People in surrounding villages had stopped visiting the shrine because a group of dacoits had killed the priest, desecrated the shrine and started using it as their campsite. It was said goddess Durga had shown her displeasure by abandoning the shrine and forsaking the people there as well. Local tribal folks say that their headman had seen a beautiful woman, statuesque, striding up the hill one night and sitting on the peak in a meditative pose. Even from below the hill he could see two tiny balls of fire in her eyes. At the break of dawn she arose and stretched her arms high above herself. In an instant she was transported away towards the sliver of orange appearing on the horizon. Moments later they saw a tiger emerge from the shrine and walk into the forest. That was many years ago.

There were many tiger tales in the villages. Every family had its own favourite tale to tell. The story of the tiger leaving Durgadevi's shrine was one that everybody knew. It had reached the city relatives as well. As boys my friends and I would pack a light meal of avalakki and bananas and trek to a stream inside the forest. We took off our clothes and jumped in. The stream was not deep enough for swimming. We could only splash about in a liberated burst and invent some catching games. We lay in the warm sun for a while, chatting and joking about each other's nakedness. We dressed, had the picnic snack and trekked back home, the friendship bonds strengthened once more.

I went there by myself this time. It had been some years, but I traced the steps to the shrine and the path into the forest quite easily. I bathed in the stream, lay in the warm sun, remembering fondly the picnic outings as boys. I dozed off.

When the slumber lifted I felt a body next to mine. It was warm and soft. When I opened my eyes I saw a beautiful young tiger snuggled against me, its head resting on my chest. Young, but fully grown. And beautiful. I gasped, but realized I was not alarmed by the presence of the most ferocious creature in nature next to me. It was actually a new and undefined joy. The tiger opened its eyes too, and gazed tenderly into mine, assuring me that I need not avoid its gaze.

The tiger purred. It was speaking to me. I found I recognized the language. The very first words were, "You are mine." To any other mortal that would mean the tiger's claim on its next meal. I knew the words meant something else. By now, the tiger had moved an arm across my chest and was gently pushing itself closer. A leg was beginning to cross my thigh. It was a tigress. How would we humans know the difference? They are all tigers for us, and they are all ferocious beasts. It was a tigress. Very soon I sensed a sweet and mildly intoxicating scent wafting before me.

The purring continued. "I watched you in the river. I watched from behind the bushes on the other bank. I knew you were the one I was waiting for." She said she had waited long, knowing I would come along one day. Finding my voice I spoke to her. I asked if she was alone, if there was a family. She explained her ancestry. She was no garden variety tiger. She came from the stock that served goddess Durga. She explained modestly that the males from her family served the goddesses as no male gods could. Conversely, young gods served the tigresses as no ordinary tiger could. Where were they now? Dwindling and disappearing. The extinction of her line of tigers was inseparably linked to the extinction of gods. But she had waited patiently.

She knew there was hope. She saw hope in me. She nestled herself closer. Once more there was the scent surrounding us.

She stopped talking and rolled over. I stroked her from head to hip. She crouched and presented herself to me. We made love. We lay in the sun in close embrace. I had become a man in the city, but I had never experienced such purity of love in a union. We made love once again. We lay in the sun again.

I awoke and began to dress. She asked where I was going. I was hoping she would not. I said it was time to go home. Home? Wasn't this my home, she asked. I replied I could come again. It was a sincere reply. I saw the beginnings of disappointment in her. And anger. I had no way of explaining what it meant to go home, to go back to my people, back to work in the city and back to being... I could not complete the sentence. Being human. I was not sure myself what that meant now. Or whether it was important. I simply said it was time to go. She asked softly if there was somebody else. The truth was that my parents had found a girl in the next village they wanted me to consider. I had seen her in a community wedding, but had not really known her. But the truthful answer to the question now was no, there was nobody else. Then why was I letting her down? She paused and added, deceiving her. Whatever could there be in the city more pure and blissful than the union she had offered me. I had no answer. She made her final plea. She said she had chosen me because she saw that I was different from other human beasts. She had hopes of restoring sanity in a human through our union. But I was insisting on remaining stupid and blind.

I muttered that our joyous time together was the most memorable in my life and that I would never ever forget her. She repeated softly... that I would never ever forget her. She then stood on her hind legs and pronounced a curse on me. "The blessing of goddess Durga shall be a curse upon you.

You are blessed with the highest intelligence that a man may have. It will rest on you as a curse. You will never forget. You will never forget anything. You will live long. Your body will refuse to die. But you will be crippled the rest of your life with unending memory that remains indelible. You will forget how to forget. Go now and live your unforgetting life. The goddess has spoken." Those were her last words to me. I watched for a while as she retreated into the forest, and then hurried back to the village myself.

End of story.

⁂

Chief Information Officer. The figure returned to the city and resumed work. It was in the company that had given him his first job. He had stayed on because they had treated him well. They treated him well because he was so dependable. There was nothing he did not know about processes and procedures, about past incidents and precedence. People came and went, each new person wondering what the correct procedure was and often reinventing it. The company soon learned that they simply had to refer all queries to him. He had it all there in his head. He was dependable. It was his infallible memory. He rose quickly to become the Chief Information Officer. He was happy that he could serve the company in the only way he could.

Sometimes he wished the day never ended. He could stay in the office forever. Outside work hours it was a very difficult life indeed. Every step he took, every sound he heard and every little leaf flitting in the breeze would trigger great floods of memories. It was a brain reformatted. The vast underground reservoir for storing sense data and their associations had been let loose. It had ceased to remain underground. Every bit of data acquired through life was whizzing about in a gigantic and monstrously efficient Random Access Memory, awake all the time. He had learned not to look around too much, and to keep his eyes closed most times. It eased the flood, but did not stop the flow of sensory data from the past that served no purpose.

He wandered on, day to day, year to year. It was many long years. He remembered the exact number of years and days that he had been a wanderer. Nobody else knew.

The figure put his head down once more, resting. Did Sanjay wish to know anything else? He was not sure. The figure spoke for him yet again and asked if Sanjay had ever wondered about his own job and career and where it was heading. On and off, he replied. Sanjay had realized that in the woefully crowded space of his job as a techie the surest formula for steady progress in the company was to stay in sync with the giant machine. There was no scope for people like him to even think of anything original. And yet, any big lift came from a breakthrough algorithm. It had to be something completely out of the ordinary. It had also to be elegantly simple in design, when you come to think of it. Did he have any ideas? Not until a few minutes ago, Sanjay confessed. It could be in the transfer mechanisms of human memory. The figure revealed a hint of interest and asked if it was he that Sanjay was thinking of. Yes, it was in cybernetics. If we could work on a process for a ready two-way flow of data... a trapdoor switch that let in vast amounts of hidden data into the consciousness and sent them back when the purpose was served.

"You are wondering if you can learn from my experience..."

"Yes, how can I turn your curse into a gift?"

"Well, I can gift it to you."

"In what way?"

"I know that I can pass on what I am carrying to only one person in the whole world."

"And that person is...?

"That person could be you. I believe it is you."

"What makes you think so? That it could be me?"

"Why else would I have chosen you for this visit?"

Sanjay felt a sense of confidence swelling in him. He asked how they might proceed. The figure turned the chairs to face each other. He placed his palms on Sanjay's temples and closed his eyes. He asked Sanjay to do the same and remain silent for a while. He then asked Sanjay to invite Mother Durga into his home. All available knowledge would flow from him to Sanjay after that.

When Sanjay opened his eyes the figure was at the door, seeking permission to leave and thanking him for the hospitality. Sanjay wanted to say that it was he who was thankful, but before he could speak the figure had vanished.

In state of tremulous excitement Sanjay sat again to meditate and test his memory. He wanted to see how far back he could go. He tried to reconstruct details of his first school. It worked. He was in the classroom. He saw the mango wood desks, ink stained, and the names of girl students engraved with pocket knives. The blackboard had the overnight home-work scribbled on it. The room was empty. Sanjay had arrived early because it was his turn to clean the board, straighten the desks and benches, and empty the waste basket. The watchman was drawing water from the well outside. The rhythmic sound from the iron pulley stopped after a while. It meant it was almost seven in the morning. The school bell would ring in a minute.

He went further back to see himself as an infant on his mother's lap. He saw a moon smiling down at him, a large vermillion dot on the forehead. He felt her warmth. She was singing her favourite lullaby. It was Yashoda scolding her adopted baby Krishna for stuffing himself with dollops of stolen butter. She did it ever so lovingly, wiping his face with the edge of her sari.

Could he go back even further? Could he see his birth? Oh yes, he could. It was in a forest. He lay on a bed of straw in a clearing. A tigress was suckling him dotingly. A crackling static appeared, the scene turned hazy. He meditated with greater calm, breathing deeply. The sounds returned, but the sights were blanked out. He heard footsteps in the distance, trampling twigs and dried leaves. There were excited voices. He felt the tigress pick him up and take him to a secluded spot. A fragmented picture reappeared briefly. She dragged a small fallen branch, still leafy, and placed it over him. She licked his face once and withdrew. The sounds faded out.

Blackout.

The Last Cheetah

My grandfather was a hunter. That is how my friends in school knew me, Cheenu, grandson of a hunter. He is still alive. If you walk down Seventeenth Cross in the evening between six and seven, you will see him seated in a wheelchair in the first floor balcony facing the street. You can't miss the house. It is the only two-storeyed building in that stretch, the figure 1952 decoratively embossed on the balcony front. All the other houses in this old area of Bangalore have been knocked down and replaced by five and six-storeyed apartment blocks. It is still called a residential area, but everybody knows that at least two apartments in each block are offices of commercial outfits. The cars parked on both sides of the roads have drivers, snoozing with their seats tilted fully back.

That is his evening outing nowadays. One hour in the balcony before he is wheeled back and given his evening medication and rub down. He gets to the balcony with a walker. It is a struggle. He moves very slowly, but the walk from his room to the balcony is his persistent demand. Once there he is helped into the wheelchair by the caregiver. The walker is folded flat and fixed to the back of the wheelchair. An hour later he is wheeled back to his room. The first ten minutes after he is brought to the balcony is the best time to see him. He has a faint smile on his face. You can wave to him and greet him from the street. Many do that. He will nod his head gently, twice, raise his wrist from his lap and wave back. He looks regal seated in the balcony. It could be the height, a good fifteen feet above the road, looking down at the common folk there in his evening durbar. He is less responsive after fifteen minutes and quite unresponsive after half past six. His eyes are open, but he is looking through you at the great beyond.

His morning outing is also an hour, but we don't see him then. He is taken to the park in the car, wheeled to a clearing within a cluster of old rain trees where the morning sun is allowed in to greet him exclusively. He must get a lot of sunshine, preferably the morning sun, the doctors said. No durbar here, except the occasional wood pigeon and mynah. A Labrador retriever drops by at times to pick up the ball thrown from the other side of the park. He sniffs Grandpa's ankles, prostrates himself before him, slapping his tail on the grass three times, and hops along with the ball retrieved. A gun dog by ancestry, he knows a hunter when he sees one.

The Rajah of Surguja shot down hundreds of cheetahs in Madhya Pradesh. He also killed god knows how many tigers and leopards! And bears and crocodiles and even wild elephants. It was called Central Provinces then. While some rajahs bred cheetahs as hunting leopards, some others loved to gun them down in the wild. The Rajah of Surguja was one of them. They say he shot the last cheetah in India some time in 1947. That is not true. It was my grandfather who shot the last cheetah. It was in 1954 in the month of September. I should know. I have the skin of that cheetah, gifted to me by grandpa. He told me the story himself. It was in this very park, on a morning walk, just he and I.

It was in those days when he took in the morning sun walking, not seated in a wheelchair. He also said he wasn't sure how much longer he would be able to enjoy the walk in the park, and that he had so many stories to tell, so much that had remained untold.

For over a year the cheetah skin was hung on the wall in my study room. I liked to see it there when I returned from college late in the evening and switched on the light. I didn't have the heart to take it off the wall, but it had to be done. My father's friend was a police officer. His firm advice was that it should be hidden somewhere and nobody should know about the skin. It was not safe to display it, we could get into trouble.

⌘ ⌘ ⌘ ⌘ ⌘

My grandfather was not really a hunter. He could not have been one. Not with a name like Narasimhachar. They called him Achar in the village. Or Achar sir, or Acharji. In the family he was Narasimha. He wore his caste mark on the forehead all the time, a good Vaishnavite trident, refreshing it every morning after his bath. On important occasions, such as a wedding in the village, he wore a Mysore turban as well. The family liked to call him a hunter. I never knew if it was with pride or in jest. I didn't care. I liked being known as the grandson of a hunter.

Grandpa was a farmer, really. He was the field officer of an extension centre run by the State government that provided services to farmers in far off places with no connection to the cities. There was a small number of service centres in the State, each centre serving many villages around it in the taluk. The field officers were not farmers themselves, but knew enough about farming, seeds, sowing, harvesting and animal husbandry and dairying and elementary veterinary practice to make themselves useful to the villages. They were respected by the villagers and sometimes held in awe. The field officer's house was the only one in the entire taluk that had a gun in it. The only others who had guns were the wandering dacoits. They left the villagers of this taluk in peace. They were too poor. It was only in the mango season that the occasional emissary dropped by. If he was lucky there would be some wild pig meat to take back.

There were two guns kept locked in a specially built almirah in an inner room. Both were of English make, revered, not country models. Both were shotguns, acquired when the British administered the districts. One was a standard double-barreled breach loading 12 bore ("Dubby" as the Anglo-Indian Deputy Commissioner called it) and the other was the smaller 16 bore.

Grandpa taught me many things. Once on a night camp he taught me all about the stars in the sky and how to find directions by watching the stars. I was amazed at the number of stars we could see when we left the city behind. He also told me why a shotgun is called a shotgun, and how it is different from a rifle.

He explained how the bigger number was actually a smaller bore. The shot in the 12 bore was one-twelfth of a pound, and in the 16 bore it was one-sixteenth of a pound. I figured out by myself what that was in grams. Ah, yes, the 16 gauge copper wire is thicker than the 20 gauge. There were three types of ammunition stocked. The first was called the slug or the single ball, meant for big game, especially the tiger. It was hardly ever used. The second was buckshot. It came in two sizes, the LG, holding six pellets inside the cartridge, and the SG, with nine pellets.

The LG was popular because it was good for both wild pigs and boar and the other big cat in the jungle in these parts, the panther. There was no birdshot ammunition. Shooting birds was a cowardly act in the villages. There were over two hundred pellets in one shot that spread out to the size of a bullock cart wheel, so that at least one hits the bird! It was sinful. And shooting snakes was unthinkable.

Grandpa had learned very early that snakes are as scared of us as we are of them. They get out of our way as soon as they sense footsteps heading their way. Except the Russell's viper. A ziddi by nature, the viper stands his ground defiantly, daring the human to cross his path. Too bad if you had a brush with a Russell's viper. It was a fifty-fifty chance of your being saved.

There were snakes everywhere in the village, and you learned to walk with the right kind of stride, and you carried the right kind of stick to deal with them. You never hit them with the stick, of course. You used it get them out of the way.

Hunting by the field officers was forbidden. The gun could be used only under a small number of out of the ordinary circumstances. These were listed in the Service Standing Orders and Operating Procedures and had the strictest definitions. One of them was crop damage by marauding animals, such as wild pigs. They came in the mango season. In the old days the guns would be kept on a table in the verandah when the District Collector came to the centre on an inspection tour. The carton of ammunition was displayed next to the guns. Eley-Kinoch was the standard supply, the red and green casings fitted flush into the rimmed brass caps. The display made the revenue collection from the farmers smoother. And quieter.

Grandpa gave me a handful of spent cartridges. He put them in a biscuit tin and stuck a label on top that said For Dear Cheenu. The cartridge shells were kept upright in my bookshelf in two neat, tight rows. They were more awe inspiring than the little framed picture of Raghavendra Swamy that aunt Kamala had given me for the bookshelf. I put that picture on the small bedside table. Aunt Kamala was satisfied and pleased.

After the Great War the white man's presence in the districts dwindled rapidly. The guns remained. They were now serviced by the nearest District Police Station. An armourer would be sent out once a month to inspect the weapons, oil and clean the barrels, check the ammunition stock and make the necessary entries in a leather bound register. Another regular was the crop inspector, who brought with him the DDT spray.

It was a fortnightly spray at first, but he soon turned it into a weekly visit, proclaiming the spray the greatest boon to mankind since the steam locomotive. The villagers understood the power of coal, they did not understand steam power or, for that matter, the spray. They had members of the family working in the coalfields not too far from their villages. Most had never traveled by train, but had taken a ride to Nagpur to see them at the railway station. It meant a whole day's outing, an hour and a half by bullock cart to the District road and over two hours by bus from there to Nagpur city.

On the way there were three railway crossings. They loved it when the crossing was closed, piling out of the bus to watch the train hurtling by. A visit to the tent cinema close to the bus station was the mandatory pilgrimage before returning exhausted and exhilarated to the village.

⁂

When the young Narasimha returned to the village with his bride from Bijapur, he had the villagers enthralled with stories of their day and night train ride from one State to another. Not only was there a bullock cart waiting for him, a convoy of four more carts was at the dusty road where the bus from Nagpur dropped them.

The women took over and helped Vatsalabai settle in quickly. They gave her a guided tour of the village, took care of the milk and butter supply to the house, arranged for extra coal for the kitchen and taught her to make jowar bhakri. They showed her how to tell a god-sent cobra from the evil viper, the devil's agent. They introduced her to the Nageshwari shrine at the edge of the village. Vatsala made it a practice to visit the shrine at least once a week after that.

One evening, returning from the shrine, Vatsala noticed the usually sedate langur apes in an animated state. They were darting across treetops, crying out hoop-hoop, the still air making the hoops sound so much louder. She didn't know what it was that made her do it, but she found herself walking faster, heading straight home instead of stopping by the well to toss in the handful of flowers. Reaching home she asked Narasimha about the excited langurs. Pandu must be back, he said, adding that it was a good thing she came straight home.

Pandu was the name given to the cheetah spotted now and then in the taluk. He was also known as the eccentric one, the wandering monk, the one who was seen in many different places at different times, always by himself. His mate was not seen as often, but was thought to be the bread winner of the family. She went out for the kill whenever needed, leaving Pandu with his meditation. People often wondered whether Pandu and his mate had any offspring. Nobody had ever seen any cheetah cubs in the taluk. Why not, they wondered. The women in the village had a different explanation. They thought Pandu and his mate must have decided not to have babies. What sort of world was left for them to live in?

The boys in the village were the first to notice something wrong. The mango season was on time, and they were at them after school and the day's household chores. But they tasted different. So did the sugarcane. The grown-ups didn't pay them any attention. The boys were always imagining things. Besides it was time for the first mango party of the season. They went to Acharji's house to invite him and Vatsalabai to the party.

It was all nicely connected. The first basket of mangos was always sent to grandpa. This year there was Vatsalabai as well, so it was a special consignment. Outside their kitchen was a pit for dumping the mango skins and stones. That attracted the wild pigs. It was reported by the villagers as crop damage. Grandpa was allowed to take action and shoot a pig or two for this criminal behaviour of the pigs. The villagers gathered at night in a clearing in the nearby woods. While the pigs roasted on a low fire spit the villagers sat all around the fire, eating mangos, singing and breaking into dance as the night progressed. The local mahua brew helped. The mangos were the local juicy variety called Chusni, to be squeezed and sucked, not sliced. By the end of the party there would be two huge mounds of empty mango skins, one on the janana side and one on the mardana side.

When the boys came to see Narasimha he admitted to them that he had noticed it too. There was more to it, he thought. He had seen a full grown cobra slithering away, but at half its usual speed. And when he raised the gun to shoot the wild pig he thought it was unsteady on its feet, swaying a bit, as if it had indulged in some of the local brew itself. The most unusual sight was the krait lying on a rocky patch in the daytime as if it was sunning itself. Everybody knows that the krait is a nocturnal serpent, never spotted at daytime. What was it doing out there at ten in the morning in that stuporous state?

Grandpa told me that he had no way of proving anything. After all, the spray came from important government officials. It was known that they had received it as a gift to India from countries that had won the great World War.

⁂

Narasimha and Vatsalabai were seated under the old neem tree in front of the house. They often had an evening chai there, watching the sun go down behind the hills in the distance. They saw a small group of villagers striding up. Here it comes, another crop damage, he murmured. The villagers had come to him with a different story this time. It was a cheetah.

Grandpa told me the story in full detail in one of our walks in the park. A fully grown calf had been killed and dragged to a spot in the middle of the woods. The villagers insisted that he simply had to kill the cheetah. They were furious. Every cow and calf was precious in every household. He tried to explain the rules and regulations laid down about using the guns for any big cat.

They were unimpressed. Their counter argument was drawn from natural law. It was the nature of the cheetah to drag a fresh kill to a secluded spot and leave it there. This was done after a ritual first small helping. It was the nature of the cheetah to return to the kill after a day for a second leisurely helping. It would be a perfect opportunity to shoot the beast, preoccupied with its butcher duties. In fact some of them were already setting up two machans on the trees facing the kill.

Reluctantly and not without some trepidation Grandpa headed indoors to take out old Dubby from its almirah. Grandma Vatsalabai went into the puja room. He put on his jacket, thrust a handful of cartridges into the pocket, and picked up his trusty four-cell flashlight, all in one swift but shaky set of moves. He stepped out of the house and asked the men to lead the way. Wishing to keep the number small, only three of them accompanied grandpa into the woods. There would be two each on the two machans. The three men carried lathis, which was less than reassuring. One of them had a large carving knife slung on one side. The motley group marched single file towards the woods, grandpa bringing up the rear. Grandma had assured him that she would remain in the puja room till the party returned from its expedition.

The sun was down by the time the party entered the woods. Visibility dropped rapidly to just about ten feet. The men advised grandpa not to use the flashlight. He knew they had arrived at the machan when the air was filled with the stench of the rotting carcass. The machans were ready. The men had thoughtfully created make-shift rungs for the party to climb up. They seemed certain that the wait would not be longer than an hour or two. They gave grandpa a leg-up and left the scene. The darkness was thick now. Four men in place on two machans, waiting...

Grandpa remembered being told during his training that the movement of the big cats through the forest is silent because of their padded feet. He now wondered how they would know if the cheetah had arrived. What would be the sign? Just as he thought of whispering the question to his companion, he was tapped gently on the shoulder and told that the cheetah was near the kill, circling it before settling down for the feast. Grandpa put his hand in his pocket, took out two cartridges, slipped them into the two barrels and closed the breach. The butt at the shoulder and the barrel half raised, he waited for a proper sighting. At last he could see the full outline of the beast, his left side presented to the machan. Grandpa raised the gun and squeezed the first trigger. There was a sickening click. Grandpa cursed his luck that he should have a misfire at this most important moment. The cheetah, alerted by the click, took a step to the side, looked up at the machan and began to retreat when grandpa's companion turned on the flashlight, hoping to stop the beast in its tracks. Grandpa fired the second shot. It worked this time. But they saw the cheetah leap into the thickness of the woods on the left. Silence.

There was a pow wow across the two machans. Grandpa was willing to admit that he was no hunter and that it was a bad shot. They should go home.

The villagers were sure that the cheetah had been hit and that it could easily be tracked down and killed. That was the worst news grandpa had heard in all his years in the village. The Standing Orders were very clear on the matter. No big cat was to be ever fired at and left wounded, as it could turn a man-eater. It was the sole responsibility of the person causing the wound to find the animal and kill it, with all the attendant dangers of getting face to face with a wounded big cat. It also meant bearing all the costs of organizing a hanka, which was a large contingent of men with country weapons, beating drums and all, to drive the animal to a clearing and then shooting it.

The villagers insisted on pursuing the mission. They won, not surprisingly. They climbed down to the ground cautiously. Grandpa opened the breach to reload. Damn, the first barrel had a 16 bore cartridge lodged well inside the breach. In his hurry to fill his pocket he had not checked the cartridges carefully, and the odd 16 had got mixed with the 12 bore cartridges. Grandpa accepted his fate stoically. He loaded the one available barrel and waited for the others to lead the way again. They were clear that it was grandpa who had to be at the head of the line, as he had the gun. They won again.

Into the thick woods went the foursome, taking one cautious step after another, grandpa leading, the occasional encouraging word from one or the other behind. At least they were there with him. Grandpa mumbled his gratitude to the lord above for small mercies. He had his gun at the ready, but was wondering all the time how long this crouched and agonizingly slow trek would take. On the other hand it would be a relief if it went on till daybreak. Then they could all go home and worry about the hanka later. There was a lull in the conversation, the men not knowing whether to talk or stay silent. About twenty feet in front and to the right they heard the crack of twigs on the ground, followed by a blood curdling snarl. Grandpa turned in the direction and fired. His companion turned on the flashlight. It was there on the ground, felled by grandpa's LG, writhing. It was actually as close as fifteen feet. With a new found determination grandpa reloaded and fired, reloaded and fired. He emptied a total of five LGs in the direction of the beast till it stopped moving. It was done. The villagers raised a victory cry: Jai Hanuman!

One of them took out his matches, lit a dried twig, and burnt the cheetah's whiskers. It was believed that the big cat's whiskers were highly poisonous and were used to dispatch one's enemies by grinding it and secretly mixing it in their food. The one with the knife began to skin the animal immediately. The next day he rubbed it with salt and hung it up to be dried in front of grandpa's verandah, stretched fully on a bamboo frame. It made a pretty sight against the sun, the light shining through the sixteen holes. When people ask me about the holes in the cheetah skin in my room I change the topic deftly. How could I possibly explain?

Two days later when grandpa and grandma Vatsalabai were at their evening chai under the neem tree they heard the unmistakable low snarl of a cheetah behind the barn on the side, the sound of sawing wood. It was the mate.

It had tracked down its missing partner. They hurried indoors and bolted the doors. Through the parted curtain of the window they saw the mate stepping out from behind the barn, pausing, and walking away. This happened the next two evenings as well. When the villagers heard about the visit they pleaded with grandpa to shoot it down. It would be an easy target. He refused firmly. This time he won. The cheetah stopped the evening visits after the third time.

My grandfather actually shot the second last cheetah. It was the female. The last cheetah was the surviving mate who died of loneliness, wandering through the hills, denying himself food and drink and breathing his last in a pit half filled with moldy leaves and leeches.

❖ ❖ ❖ ❖ ❖

The Retriever hopped into the clearing in the park chasing the ball. He went up to the wheelchair and sniffed at the footrest as he was accustomed to. He then started barking, raising an alarm. The wheelchair was empty. The walkers and joggers went about their routines not noticing anything unusual. Then an elderly couple came along. They remembered grandpa on the wheelchair and went up to the barking Retriever. They were joined by the driver who had taken a tea break. The three of them asked many passers-by about grandpa. An old rag-picker sleeping on the stone bench half raised himself and told the group that he had seen the aged gentleman rising from the wheelchair and stretching his arms to the sky. He then took a folding walker from the back of the wheel chair and hobbled away, ever so slowly, as if that was what he had to do. The rag-picker turned and was going back to sleep. Did he remember where he went? Which direction? Of course. He walked in the direction of the little pond in the wooded area, beyond the banyan tree. It was now dried up and the pit was filled with moldy leaves.

• • •

The Gift

The thing you remembered most about Ravi was his smile. People who study people, like actors and psychologists and stage hypnotists, not to forget godmen and conmen, these people will tell you that a smile is inseparable from the text beneath the smile. The smile is part of our language, you could say landscape, always saying something. They will tell you that there are at least twelve distinct categories of smiles. When two or three motives combine to produce a smile, as they usually do, you have a near infinite variety of smiles. Ah, but as we grow up and learn the ways of the world, we lose most of our smiles, so to speak, and narrow down our repertoire to a rather predictable three or four. The boring three or four. They also say that no two smiles are the same, even within a person. That is because no two experiences are the same. Ah, but as we grow up and learn the rules of the game, we apply the principle of Economy of Force. We reduce all experiences to a manageable few and manage them with three to four smiles. That is what growing up is all about. Ravi's delight in smiling was more precious to him than mastery over the ways of the world. He chose to stop growing up.

There were some things Ravi did well and loved doing. Gardening was one of them. Embroidery, weaving mats and moulding candles in many shapes and colours were others. The instructors liked Ravi because he could be left alone in the occupational training workshop for any length of time. He needed no supervision. If you passed by him he would look up with a smile and return to the task immediately. He always hummed to himself when he was working. He did not sing. He only hummed tunes, and it was with a sweetness of sound that neutralized the annoyance from the cars honking outside. The humming seemed to go so naturally with the smile. He never sang the words.

Ravi had a sister, Ramya, who was three years older. There were five pictures of Ramya in the living room, taken over five birthday parties from age two to age eighteen. The sixth was with her husband on her wedding day. There were at least fifteen pictures of Ravi between the living and dining areas, including one made into a fridge magnet. He smiled at you from every direction. There was one large frame with the whole Pai family of four in the picture. It had Ravi and Ramya standing behind Sridevi, their housewife-mother, and Dr. Manohar Pai, the physician-father. The other large frame had only Ravi's face, his beatific smile beaming at a spot above and behind your head. The picture was placed above the entrance to the puja room. Under the picture were the words:

RECALLED FOR A HIGHER PURPOSE.

⁂ ⁂ ⁂ ⁂ ⁂

Mr. Narayanasami Mudaliar, better known as Sami in the community, was an entrepreneur-technocrat who had built a successful electronics business, manufacturing customized special purpose peripherals. He was also called Transformer Sam or TranSam or just Sam in Rotary circles. This was not the first time the media had done a story on Sami.

"He first came here when he was about sixteen. It was a short visit arranged by the Institute. I had set up a lunch after the tour of the workshop, and I wanted the other apprentice-trainees to get to know Ravi in a relaxed, informal setting. We knew he loved ice cream. We had a large brick of butterscotch brought to the table. You should have seen his face!"

The news magazine had hand-picked Dr. Vatsala Jain, a well informed and senior sociologist, to do the story.

"Mr. Mudaliar, you have appeared in many interviews before. Your business success is widely admired. In this interview we wish to cover your support to charity. We can do that with a focus on Ravi." The focus on Ravi...

Sami had the milestones in his life clearly charted even when he was in the government engineering college. An internship of a year in an electrical engineering factory, followed by front office experience in his uncle's agency business, and he would be ready to start a small industry himself. He would marry after he had made his first million. He would be a one crore company by the time his first child went into pre-school. He would have a house of his own well before the second child, large enough to have his parents stay with them. They would have a cottage in Kodaikanal. Sami's wife, Andal, was not only the complete homemaker, she helped Sami with the business, crossing the five million milestone ahead of time. Andal introduced Sami to the world of charity. A Masters in social work herself, she worked as a volunteer twice a week for three hours at the Institute. It was she who suggested that Ravi might be given the opportunity of occupational placement in Sami's business. It didn't have to be at the factory. It could be at the prototype workshop in the out-house at the back.

⌘ ⌘ ⌘ ⌘ ⌘

When Ravi was about four his mother decided that it was time for a second opinion. It was a Saturday and Manohar was away at the Municipal Market for the weekly shopping. Sridevi was at home with Ravi, working on the brunch menu. When the front door rang Sridevi knew it was the Speed Post. As she was signing her name she heard a sharp scream from the kitchen. Rushing in she saw a trail of blood going into the study. Ravi was seated on his favourite modha, bent, holding his left hand tightly in his right. In a flash Sridevi was at Ravi's feet. Her instinct told her that a tight hug had to come before any words to show her own concern.

"Ravi! What happened?" she asked after a few moments. Ravi looked up and held out his cut index finger, still held in his right hand. And just a second later he smiled. Sridevi hugged him again. It was a joy that had no precedence. But over his shoulder she was wide-eyed in wonder. He was smiling... Did he feel no pain? Should he not be howling? Will he hurt himself easily?

That evening Sridevi decided to talk to Manohar. From the first time they had been alerted about Ravi, Manohar was not saying much, except that it might have been worse. She insisted that she was not in denial. It was important to have a correct and full picture, as it would help with the correct line of action. Manohar did not disagree. He would arrange for a visit to a specialist clinic. An appointment was taken for a first meeting.

On the way back home from the clinic, Sridevi stopped at the pavement fruit shops to buy some fresh grapes that had just come into the market. When she was making the payment she noticed that Ravi had stepped over to the fortune teller under the tree. "Ravi!" she called in controlled annoyance. Seated on his haunches, Ravi turned and smiled. So did the fortune teller. He had a large wooden cage before him which housed two green parakeets in separate compartments. Next to the cage was a neat bundle tied in a satin scarf. Sridevi joined Ravi, deciding to allow him the afternoon entertainment.

Opening the bundle with a brief ceremony, the fortune teller explained that there were twenty seven cards, representing the Indian cosmic system. The cards carried images of Hindu deities. Would madam like to know what the future held for the handsome young lad seated before him? Why not, she thought, catching Ravi's expectant looks, now beaming in delight. The fortune teller asked Ravi to choose a parakeet. Ravi chose one without hesitation. "Aah..." exclaimed the fortune teller, "A boy with a clear mind!" He then opened the cage and let the chosen parakeet out. The parakeet stood before the set of cards, now spread like a Chinese fan before Ravi. He instructed Ravi to place both his hands before the cards, palms facing down, fingers spread, such that the positive energies from his soul might flow unhindered to all the cards. Taking a deep breath the fortune teller posed a question to the parakeet in a sing-song voice. He asked if Ravi's past life could be found in the cards. The parakeet nodded a Yes readily. And his future life? The parakeet nodded again.

The fortune teller closed his eyes and placed the fingertips of both his hands on Ravi's temples humming a long "Ommm..." He then recited a short verse in the same sing-song voice, giving the parakeet the necessary mandate to reveal Ravi's past. The parakeet walked over to the cards, paused for a second, and instead of picking one of the cards, climbed up Ravi's extended right hand and perched itself on his shoulder. Ravi whooped in joy. Sridevi, just slightly alarmed, stood by with a rescue plan if needed. Ravi smiled at the parakeet, which returned the gesture with a friendly nibble on Ravi's right ear.

Never before had the fortune teller seen anything like this, never heard of anything like this in the whole community of fortune tellers. "Madam, this boy!" He was ecstatic. "This boy, your son, is no ordinary mortal being! He is destined for a greatness that cannot be described by any of the cards here, madam!" He refused to take any money for the consultation.

⌘ ⌘ ⌘ ⌘ ⌘

Ravi smiled a new smile when he was introduced to the bench set up in the Institute's workshop. There were three other trainees with him. On the bench were four small wooden frames the size of small shoe boxes. They were bolted to the table top. The boxes were open at the top and front and had a small crank handle on one side. There were rolls of shiny golden red wire kept in cartons behind the bench. All of these new sights made some of the trainees nervous. Not Ravi.

The trainees were seated before the four boxes and shown how to crank the handle with the right hand while feeding a length of wire with the left. The wire came in different thicknesses, and had to be wound on bobbins of different sizes fitted inside the box. Getting the right hand to obey the left was not easy. Or the other way round. While the other trainees at the bench frowned and snorted or thumped the table in frustration, Ravi smiled wider. He thumped the table in delight and pressed on.

The Institute had received a donation for an Electronics Section from the industrialist, Narayanasami Mudaliar. He was willing to take components produced in the Institute for the transformers and stabilizers manufactured in his factory. Within six months of his introduction to the bench Ravi was not only turning out coils of various sizes wound to perfection, he had mastered the art of stripping wire ends and soldering them to printed circuit boards. There were three gold stars under his name on the notice board. Always the first at the bench, even on Mondays, he was already arranging parts in the correct order in an arc left to right while the soldering iron was heating up.

Ravi noticed some excited chatter at the front office. A large car had drawn up and the Institute staff had streamed out of the office, led by the director herself, to greet the visitor. The smartly dressed chauffer went around the car and opened the door for the visitor to step out. The soldering iron was ready and it was time to start on the first assembly, but Ravi could not help looking a little longer. It was Mr. Mudaliar. As the director stepped forward to greet him the chauffer went to the door on the off side and held it open. It was Sridevi. Ravi gasped in joy. "Amma!" She hadn't said anything about coming to the Institute when he left home in the morning. Just then the instructor entered the workshop and asked Ravi to follow him to the Visitors Room. Reluctant to stop even as he had just begun, Ravi smiled an acknowledgement and joined the instructor. Not before switching off the soldering iron.

There was a round of clapping as Ravi entered the room. The ceremony was brief. The director made the formal announcement that Ravi would be leaving the Institute. Ravi looked up at Amma, puzzled. She squeezed his hand in the language he understood. He smiled. Mr. Mudaliar thanked the Institute for having faith in his experiment, and in the same breath he announced an annual grant to take care of an expanded workshop. There was more clapping, followed by tea and snacks and a pineapple cake, cut jointly by Mr. Mudaliar and Ravi. Paper plates and tissues in hand, Mr. Mudaliar and Amma sat on either side of Ravi and explained that he had been chosen to work for five hours a day at the design workshop in the out-house in Mr. Mudaliar's bungalow. He was getting to be seventeen now. He could do so much more in the workshop that was not possible at the Institute.

When Sami rose to fetch himself another helping of the uppuma, Sridevi leaned and whispered "So, what do you say about Draupadi?" A shy smile.

Ravi was always fond of stories from the Mahabharata. From about the time he was eight he would often ask Sridevi about Draupadi's husbands. Amma would ask teasingly if he wanted five wives. What about five parents, Ravi would ask in return. Why not, Sridevi would reply. This had become the standard close of play every time the Mahabharata stories were told at bed time. Ravi kept his plate down and hugged Sridevi. There was a muffled "Amma" against her sari that only Sridevi heard.

She whispered into his ear again: "We can do with four parents for a start, hmmm?" Two vigorous nods against the sari. "Do you think you are ready to spend half a day in your new home?" Three vigorous nods. Sridevi patted his head in a way she never had in seventeen years. Ravi buried his head in a little deeper. He could feel in the way Amma's hand moved that this was something new. In a flash he sat up again. It was a smile Sridevi had not seen before, not in seventeen years.

⌘ ⌘ ⌘ ⌘ ⌘

Sami made the announcement. "Ravi is a member of this household. He is as much at home here as in his parents' home."

"His parents have been extremely understanding. They have accepted this as Ravi's second home", added Andal, serving the coffee and biscuits.

They glanced at each other. The topic had first come up at Sami's design workshop soon after Ravi's internship. Andal had asked Sridevi in the most carefully worded and sincerely affectionate manner if she and Manohar would consider Ravi being adopted.

Sam and Andal would do everything to make Ravi loved and happy. Sridevi had said nothing. She sat still and stared ahead, two tear drops at the edge of her eyelids. She did not speak a word. Andal showed great understanding by not pressing her for an answer. She poured another cup of tea for Sridevi and gently changed the topic. Sridevi picked up the cup of tea. She had not closed the topic.

This was the part the media had never covered adequately in the past. It was what the feature issue had to get right. Andal and Sami were not the only couple without a child. She tried an opener shifting the focus to Ravi's parents.

"Sridevi and the good doctor are not the only couple with a child who is, well, different."

"Do you think they do not see that he is different?" asked Andal.

"I don't know. What I meant was..."

Anadal continued, "What you should know is that they have steadfastly stayed away from applying a label to the difference. They believe that labels don't help."

Sami added how their own attachment to Ravi was because there was no label to prejudice them. They loved him for what they saw. They had declined to look at any medical profile that the Institute felt obliged to share with them.

Sami recalled how everything Ravi said was always in a single word, if at all he chose to speak. He preferred to smile instead. It was often a single syllable. And a smile. It took Sami and Andal some time to realize that Ravi's vocabulary was not inconsiderable. They had heard him say "political", for instance, and "flabbergasted" and "topsy-turvy". He seemed to have a sentence in his head, but expressed it in a word. So, how was the first day at the workshop, Sami had asked. "Discovery", he replied. Another day, Andal and Sami had some fresh lime served on the lawn, waiting for the auto rickshaw to pick up Ravi. He looked at the expanse of flower beds, spread his arms wide and said "Vibgyor". There were other times when all you heard was "hmmm" or "hmmph" or "hurr" or his trade mark whoop.

Ravi seemed to know many words connected with gardening. Compost, moisture, weeding and pruning came to him easily. He loved the colour green. At the work bench there was a strict colour code for wiring components. At first he followed instructions mechanically. One day he was told the logic behind wiring with green, that it was to make sure energy returned to earth. There was instant joy. "Earth!" Grasping the moment

Sami explained that we must always give back good things to earth. "Good!" He returned to his wiring task with renewed vigour, humming a made up tune to himself, but adding two words for the first time to a beat: "Good! Earth! Good! Earth!"

"The first time... It almost went unnoticed." Sami stopped and looked at Andal.

Vatsala Jain, the seasoned field researcher, sensed success. The interview was getting somewhere. The training manual says that is when you have to shut up and allow the person ample time. She made eye contact and nodded to show that she was with him. And Sami continued.

It seemed nothing more than a cute expression at that time, but he knew it meant something more. It was nearly two years ago. Sami was asking Andal if she was going to the veggie market with the driver. She wasn't sure if she should, she said. Sami then asked Ravi what he thought. Shouldn't Andal go? Ravi's response was an elongated figure of eight with his head.

Sami laughed and asked if that meant a No or a Yes. Mimicking Ravi's figure of eight he asked "Yes? Or no?" Ravi understood at once. Changing to a straight left and right swing he said "No". So that was it. Andal gave the driver the list of veggies to buy and sat down on the garden swing. Moments later there was a loud crash just outside the gate. Rushing there Sami and Andal found the car rammed by a van coming in from the left. The driver had extricated himself from his side, shaken but safe, but the rear door had been completely compacted to the seat. Exactly where Andal might have been seated.

Were there other such... incidents? Of course there were. That time when the Marketing Manager was having a heated argument with Sami on the floor of the design workshop. He did not agree that the company should be aiming at increasing volumes on one line of production. The market was looking for variety and choice. Sami was firm. How on earth could the staff they had turn out anything new? Without compromising on quality? The company's reputation rested on their quality. The pause in the argument might well have meant the Marketing Manager was going to walk out. There were three taps on Ravi's bench. Both men turned to see Ravi's smiling face behind a rack. He rose and stepped forward, holding three printed circuit boards in his hand, fastened to powder coated trays the size of school lunch boxes. They were identical from the inside. On the outside there were stickers that Ravi had pasted, making them colourful. And different. One had Shirdi Sai Baba, there was Mother Teresa on the second, and the third had Snoopy and Charlie Brown taking a nap under a tree. The men first laughed in politeness, then looked at each other. Sami put the circuit boards down on the bench, held up Ravi's arm and exclaimed "Yes!" A standard production line, but distinctive packaging for market segments.

The same week there was an ongoing discussion on the pros and cons of tying up with Balaji Enterprises, a small components factory that had sent out signals about being available. Tap tap tap. The group tuned towards Ravi. Up came the head, a broad grin. Up went the right hand with the soldering iron. "Cold solder" he proclaimed. Down hand, down head. Sami caught the significance of the message. The cold solder joint was weak and unreliable, likely to come apart. The company declined the offer. A month later Balaji Enterprises closed shop.

Sami loved to toss questions about the stock market to Ravi. The answers were mostly in one or two syllables. "Phoos" was common. So was "dabba". Occasionally a stock received the high rating of "Bong!" from Ravi. Once he heard Ravi say "Bamboola!" That was it. He had to unload the stock. One afternoon Ravi took a pair of scissors and cut two pages of the business paper into sixty four bits. First into two halves, then the halves into halves, and so on, two, four, eight, till he had sixty four pieces. He put the pieces into a waste basket, climbed to the top of the stepladder kept next to the mango tree and turned it upside down. The pieces floated across the lawn in the breeze and landed all over the cacti in the rock garden. Only one of them landed on a lotus leaf in the goldfish pond. Sami could see the name of the stock settled on the lotus leaf.

That night Sami had a long chat with Andal after dinner. They made up their mind. They would create a Trust and give away most of their private wealth for a charitable cause, keeping just enough for a decent life for themselves. And Ravi.

A long pause. Sami was looking out of the window. The interviewer offered a lead. Was that something like a turning point in his business? Sami first nodded 'Yes' and then turned and broke into a grin. He made an elongated figure of eight with his head. "I suppose you could call it that", he replied. The funny thing was what happened thereafter. He found that the more he gave away the more his business grew.

"Call it fate, call it divine intervention, call it chance, call it anything... It does not matter what it is called. The fact is our lives changed."

"Can you say something more about that? Change in what way?"

A short pause this time, and Sami continued. The change was obviously for the better, he was sure, although he had no way of explaining exactly how it was better. It was as if life was more complete. He had never imagined business success in these terms before. The public adoration, the respect in the marketplace, the growth and diversification, the momentum. The momentum. All of this without having to do things to be heard.

"And in your family life?" This time Sami looked Vatsala in the eye and spoke a single word. "Serene", he said softly, "something Andal and I had never known".

Vatsala wished to know more. What did this mean for the future? The future of the company, their future life? Sami surprised her by saying that she was the first person they were going to talk about this.

"We are creating another Trust. It is called the Ravi Kiran Foundation. We hope it helps to bring the gift of light and warmth into some more homes."

The Trust was conceived during the last trip the Mudaliars had made to Tirupati with Sridevi and Manohar. Vatsala had known, of course, that the four of them had been going to Tirupati together the last three years.

Before the interview concluded Sami took Vatsala around to the back and showed her the design workshop where some of the company's greatest prototypes had been developed. Andal said she would go in make the lime juice with mint that Ravi had always loved. When Sami brought Vatsala to the dining table he asked if he could be excused. Vatsala thanked him profusely, but wished to ask just one more question before Sami left. This interview was with the Mudaliars, of course, but would it be all right if she met Sridevi and Manohar for a chat as well?

"But I thought you have spoken to them already", Sami replied. Andal added that there was nothing the Pais and Mudaliars kept from each other. Vatsala explained that it was part of her professional code to let them know, so she wished to have their permission.

Andal was quick to reply on behalf of both. She appreciated Vatsala's ethical principle and admired her professional conduct. Yes, of course, she could meet Ravi's parents, but she had a question too.

"May we make a request in return?" Vatsala agreed readily. Andal looked at Sami, who signaled that she should continue.

"This request comes from our experience from the past. We find it so interesting, even amusing, that a journalist goes into an interview expecting to find something she believes is there. And then keeps looking for that something all the time."

Sami added, "...and manages to find that something in the interview even when it's not there." Vatsala tried to find words to respond. Andal continued.

"Please do make the effort to understand what we really meant in all that we have shared with you today."

Andal requested Vatsala to wait till she got some haldi-kumkum and entered the puja room. Sami thanked Vatsala once again and said he had to leave. Vatsala accompanied him to the door. She returned and stood by herself next to the rose wood dining table for ten. She noticed the large picture of Ravi placed above the entrance to the puja room. Under the picture were the words:

THE SUN RECALLED BUT THE GIFT OF SUNSHINE REMAINED.

[It is known that overall intellectual capacity is a mix of several different abilities. Among the intellectually challenged it is not uncommon for a specific ability to be manifest in an enhanced manner. There are several real life accounts of such people, some even made into movies.]

The Doorbell

As always the first sounds from the street were from the wheelbarrows. The garbage clearing squad remained punctual although the Corporation had denied them the rise in pay. It was not easy for them to strike work, the way the bus drivers had done a month ago. The street dogs greeted them with their affectionate barking. The women were heard talking to them, enquiring about their last meal. The first bus appeared soon after, honking unnecessarily, as if mocking the garbage clearing women. The street was waiting for the sun to arrive.

The first shop to open was usually the chai-bakery that served khari biscuit and bun with chai to working men on their way to early shifts. It was small, with only two tables inside, understood as reserved for the elderly. All others had their chai standing. The chai shop was housed in an abandoned building in a gully off the street. There was no other occupant in the building. It was once a large joint family. Misfortune upon misfortune had driven the older folks to death, un-cared in their last days. The younger ones had fled to the gulf or the happening cities in the south. Next to the chai shop entrance were stairs leading to a basement. The steps were narrow and steep. The basement room was where Sardar and Ranee lived.

The room had many uses day and night. Against a wall was a work table that had seen much service. It had two vises of different sizes, tools, boxes and cans of parts for repairs, and work on different projects in different stages of progress. A working stool. It revealed that Sardar Shmbhuji Lal was some kind of mechanic. In the neighbourhood he was revered as a crack handyman who fixed things for people in his basement. His day job was as a welder in a fabrication workshop.

This morning there was a '50s model table fan at the centre of Sardar's work bench. It was on and running quietly. On the stool was Sardar, bent over the table, asleep. A reluctant beam of light through a skylight window placed at street level announced that morning had broken. The street sounds gave way to the slam of a door. There was no effect on Sardar. Ranee entered, descending the rickety wooden steps. She was on her morning routine moving in and out of a room within the room partitioned imaginatively with hessian. She barely looked at Sardar as she talked. She replaced the previous day's mala on a framed photo with a fresh string of flowers.

Ranee began her news bulletin. The unfinished wall around the compound...It was getting to be a nuisance. People were dumping things there. And vagabond kids were gathering there for a smoke and using rowdy language. There was one always seated on the wall. He was there again that morning. Looked as if he hadn't gone home at all. If he had one that is. She asked Sardar when he finished She didn't think she heard him wind up. But then last night you wouldn't have heard a pack of asses braying in the room with that wedding procession outside... That boy. It was the same hideous stoop, one leg up on the wall, the other dangling, the same idiotic grin. You know, like a...like...oh well, like an idiot...She saw him on her way to the latrine. She thought she'd get there early – before the queue started – but he was there. Looked as if he had been stuck on that unfinished compound wall by the maistry to shoo the prowlers away. Or to keep off people peeing there – at least till he'd handed it over to the landlord. Or maybe the shops were closed and he couldn't get the pumpkin and chillies to hang up, and decided on a substitute. Not a nice way to start the day. The wall...it was getting to be a nuisance.

She stopped to look at the thin cotton mattresses on the floor and admonish Sardar. You could at least put your own bedding away. Look at them, like two bloody graves. You could put an inscription on the floor. Here they lie, side by side, united till the end of time. She rolled up the beddings and put them away, continuing with other tidying up chores, talking all the time. United! Ooh! You know, it could have been the same with all those emperors. Shah Jahan for instance. You think he really and truly doted on that Mumtaz as we are told? He was a bloody schemer for all we know. An operator, like any other ruler. All he wanted was something to be remembered by. And who cares who paid for it! Then that woman must have insisted on joining him on his tours and travels, on being seen by his side. And a lot of her being seen. A great embarrassment that must have been, what with at least a dozen other females screaming their heads off in protest, and threatening to leak out stories of the great Emperor's midnight pranks...You think the landlord gives us free electricity...running that fan all night? Or do I have to include switching off in my list for the morning?

When they finally knock down the building and put up a fancy apartment house, I hope they leave the basement as it is. Not just for us. I mean forever. A mausoleum concealed by a fancy apartment house. We'll ask for two simple stone slabs right here. No inscription. Just the simple slabs. It will remain a mystery. What faith were they? Were they buried here, or is it their ashes? It can become a durgah, the first basement durgah! Who knows, people might queue up to peep into this monument of eternal...of eternal...What a sight it will be outside!

She withdrew into the partitioned area, but continued in a higher pitch.

There will be three queues running every morning. One for the municipal water, one for the shithouse and the longest, grandest one for the mausoleum of Sardar and his Ranee. No, Ranee and her Sardar. It sounds more cultured that way. Don't forget my brother paid the rent for seven long years here. And my father before that for – god knows – at least three years...I don't think that compound wall will be completed though. The landlord will be dead and gone. The maistry will be rotting in his grave. We'll have just that unfinished brickwork, separating the janta from the apartment-wallas. And whatever happens, that wretch will be there, seated in the same spot, with the same stoop. The same idiotic grin...You better get your tea yourself from inside. I have more than enough on my hands today. Late by half an hour too...

Sardar stirred, adjusted his position, but remained at the table. There was a polite knock. Sardar did not respond. A shadow appeared at the window. More knocking. Sardar rose, went out to the door, taking his time about it.

"Closed. Come later. Sorry, no exceptions. Later...come tomorrow." Entering the room again he noticed the fan was switched off.

"Who put the fan off? Ranee!"

Ranee called back from inside that he had to make his own tea.

"This fan must be kept running for another hour at least! And then I must reset the bearing assembly...Where's my bedding?"

"Where it should be. On top of mine. That's about as close to..." She cut herself short.

"God, it's seven already! You think the line might have cleared by now? Maybe I could lie down for half an hour or so..."

Ranee reminded him that Ramji and his son were going to drop in that morning. Sardar mumbled a half curse. The trouble with Ramji's procession band was they were all over sixty. Buried in Shanker–Jaikishan. They hadn't learned a thing after Sangam. The same bloody tumtumtumtumtaaraaara, wedding after wedding. Worn out bloody bandwallahs playing worn out tunes on worn out instruments. Maddening! He could not concentrate. He had to redo the soldering four times. Got it done anyhow... Ramji's son...when did he say he was coming?

"Any time now. Today, tomorrow, any day."

"He's coming back loaded, no? Five years in Muscat...must have made a packet."

"Nice boy...very smart...a good boy. I knew he would do well."

Sardar chose to share his comment with the table fan. The one clever thing he did was to run away when he got the chance. Another month of idling and Ramji would have put a collar on his neck and hung a dabba drum from it, "Go on, bang it...earn your bloody meals in this house... Tumtumtumtumtarrarrarra... Bol Radhabol..."

Ranee emerged in a fresh sari, a bag in hand. She wondered if Ramji's son was bringing anything for them. Ramji, everybody knew, was hoping he'd get the new trumpet he asked for. The one he had from the army disposal must be at least two hundred years old. Sardar was not so hopeful. He knew what that Ramjikabatchha would get for Ramji...one number 2in1, one number demonstration cassette with it, and two numbers cassettes of latest jing-jang music. "As for you and me, be thankful if he remembers to visit you on his return to this street."

"Come on, he's your nephew after all."

"Hunh! Everyone in this mohalla is related to everyone else. We are all uncles and nephews.

Sardar went back to his work of tidying up at the table. Ranee stood in front of him and asked what he thought about Ramji's request? What request?

"You know what I'm talking about. He asked..."

"He asked you. He has said nothing to me."

"I told you about it as soon as..."

"Did you tell me?"

"He asked over a month ago. We talked about it the same day. You said "Hunh...we'll see". And you haven't had the time or the right frame of mind since then to say yes or no clearly."

"He's my nephew after all!"

Ranee wanted to know what that meant. What should she tell Ramji when she saw him? Sardar strode into the partitioned area. Ranee called after him, reminding him that if he did not hurry up there would be no water in the municipal tap. Sardar emerged in a lungi and vest, an aluminium mug with morning stuff in hand, and went to the door without speaking.

"One more thing. Babu asked if you could fix the petromax in his shop some time today."

Sardar barked from the door, "And one more thing. Don't try any tidying up at the work bench. Leave it as it is. Ranee looked at the table fan and echoed Sardar.

"One more thing. If you don't wipe that silly grin off your silly moon face, I'll dump you on that wall outside. Next to that drooling idiot." She smiled and gave the moon face a soft polish with the end of her sari. "He is yours for another day and night."

⌘ ⌘ ⌘ ⌘ ⌘

Ranee left for her day job, happy with the world. Sardar returned soon after, put things away inside and returned to the work bench. He tied the checked gamchha round his head, offered pranams to the bench and sat down at the stool. He meditated in silence for a minute and then started on his work, cleaning up. He talked to his friends on the work bench softly, all the mechanical devices and components on the table. He smiled and greeted them. They smiled back. They had their morning conversation.

You must know about a job he took last year. He sat down after dinner. It was about 8 o'clock. He kept all the spares, in their separate katories on his left. He laid out all the tools on his right. The fan was in front of him. Then he called Ranee. He wanted her to blindfold him. She covered his eyes with two hankies as pads, and wrapped his towel around them. He asked only for some silence after that. She moved away, spread their two beds, sat down and watched him. He sat still for about two minutes, as if in a trance, with his hands resting lightly at the edge of the table. Then he began... What can we say? The fan seemed to know his every move, his every silent instruction. It moved with him, it was one with him. When he finished, about 1 o'clock, the table was as orderly as at the start. All the tools on his right, the spares in their katories on the left, the scrap and the muck in the plastic bowl below... and a beaming, grateful, fully recovered patient before him, as he undid his blindfold.

⌘ ⌘ ⌘ ⌘ ⌘

The basement remained empty several times during the day, with Ranee away and Sardar on outdoor chores from his job at the workshop. It was never locked. This afternoon Bichhu, Ramji's son, was dropping in to look up Sardar and Ranee. With nobody answering at the street side window he let himself in. He moved slowly, exploring the room, the inner room too, and began to inspect the workbench. He picked up a half-assembled calling buzzer. Finding it fascinating, he sat at the stool, and began to examine it.

Ranee entered the basement excitedly, expecting Sardar to be there.

"They are coming. I just met Ramji on the way up. He said Bichhu had gone ahead and he'd come along soon. You'd better get moving or they'll..." She stopped abruptly, staring at Bichhu. "Who are you? Where's Sardar? What are you... wait, wait a minute! Oh, ho ho, why you're...Bichhu! Bichhu, you rascal! Why didn't you say you were...when did you...how long have you been sitting there? All by yourself? Where's Sardar, your Mama?

Bichhu explained his presence and moved awkwardly to touch Ranee's feet. She raised him and cupped his face in her hands. She joked about his newly acquired moustache, his height and his weight and his fancy pants. Bichhu could not find words to reply. Ranee reminded him of his schooldays, when he would stop on his way back and she made hot bhajiyas for him. She was sure he missed her bhajiyas. And hot jalebis on special occasions – when his gang won the cricket match. She asked if they played cricket in Muscat. They were crazy about cricket, Bichhu replied. They didn't play much themselves, but they were crazy about watching cricket.

There was a pause. They smiled, remembering his crush on her and her enjoying the attention he gave her. She asked if he ever thought of her out there. There was no time for thinking, daydreaming, anything. It was just work, work, work – from the first day of the week to the last. Lagataar work, three hundred days a year. They went to sleep on Thursdays and got up on Saturday to get back to work. Hardly any holiday. Oh yes, they got the day off when Abdul Kalam died. They slept through the morning, and did some shopping in the evening. There was a whole crowd of Indians out in the streets that evening.

Ramji and Sardar came in together. Ramji announced his entry and added that he picked up Sardar from the chai shop just before he had placed an order. Ranee dashed inside to put the tea kettle on. She peeped out from the inner room to point out Bichhu. Hadn't he grown? He was a man! Bichhu went up to Sardar to touch his feet, but was greeted instead by a warm embrace. Ramji said proudly that the first thing Bichhu wanted to do was to open a business. No more working for a contractor.

Sardar held Bichhu at arm's length and looked at him.

"You have grown. Good solid arms, working man's hands. They fed you well there?" He turned to Ramji and asked if he got the new trumpet he wanted? Ramji laughed it off.

"Oh, no! There was no time. But – ho ho – he got me such a big 2in1. And some cassettes."

At that moment Sardar looked at the work bench and was clearly annoyed. He called out to Ranee inside. "Ranee! I told you not to touch anything on the bench."

"What are you talking about? I just got in a minute ago."

"Then who...?"

Bichhu stepped forward to explain. He had picked up the buzzer and was looking at it when Ranee came in. It looked really dead and gone, he said. Sardar dropped to his knees at once, looking for a fallen part under the bench. He admonished Bichhu from down there, "It is neither dead nor gone. It has another thirty years to it at least." Bichhu asked who used a buzzer like that now? Was it worth the repair? Sardar found the fibre washer he was looking for. He knew somebody had fiddled with the assembly in his absence. As he placed all the parts of the buzzer together in one bowl, Ramji tried to return to the topic of Bichhu's business idea. Sardar was not paying attention. He spoke to Bichhu.

"As long as God keeps making fibre washers these buzzers will keep working."

"Nobody buys these anymore. It's only musical doorbells now. There is a model that plays 10 different tunes one after the other."

"How much does it cost?"

"Here, in India? Oh, about nine hundred Rupees."

"Nine hundred? You know what I'm charging to repair this buzzer? Nine Rupees. For old Udham I might even do it free."

This was an opening for Bichhu. He said he knew a way by which they could get them in kits. It would cost them about four hundred a piece. If they priced it at seven hundred, they would make two-fifty per piece. Easily two hundred nett. Maybe more. Ramji chipped in. That was a good example, he said. There were other possibilities. Who would buy them, Sardar wanted to know. Bichhu had the answer ready. In this city alone, without any special cost in advertising, his guess was, say, easily six thousand pieces in the first year.

"Six thousand new homes?"

"Not all new. Some in new homes, some replacements. About half and half."

"So, about three thousand replacements. What happens to the old ones bells, buzzers, bing bong chimes? They will be... homeless. Cast out like used matchboxes."

Ramji tried to bring the conversation to the business opportunity. It would be a humble start. In about a year they would afford an office, a peon. People can be hired to go about and sell more pieces. They could even think of fifty thousand pieces per year. Sardar looked from one to the other and asked to be heard.

"Fifty thousand, a lakh, ten lakhs. Put all the cities and towns together...Oh God, what will that number be? A great big mountain of discarded, destitute, doorbells. As high as Kalipahad in my mother's hometown."

Bichhu brought in the business proposition for Sardar. For any such business there had be a good sales plan, of course, but there also had to be good service. A good service section.

Ramji echoed Bichhu, the first thing needed was a good service section. He laid his palm on Sardar's shoulder. Sardar simply continued from where he had been interrupted.

"Just think what it means Ramji. A great big mountain of doorbells like that...how much it will have in it. How many tons of steel, how many tons of copper. And do you know there will be silver and platinum in the contact points?" Ramji shook his head and asked Sardar to focus on the conversation. Sardar kept his focus.

"Do you know the quality of the steel that goes into making those bells? Didn't you once tell me how perfect the metal must be to make your trumpet?"

Bichhu tried to be helpful and suggested that perhaps his Mamaji was thinking of another kind of business. Wasn't he? Ramji caught on. Of course! There would be good money in the scrap from discarded doorbells. They waited for Sardar to speak.

"No, nothing like that. I was just thinking why must opening a door be so costly?"

⁂ ⁂ ⁂ ⁂ ⁂

They call it an impasse. Ramji was in a hurry. Bichhu was in an even greater hurry. Sardar did not see what the hurry was all about. Ranee asked if Sardar would be a full partner. Ramjii thumped the table and said yes! Bichhu said...It depends. Sardar would need to get a head for business first. Thinking small was what Mamaji had to leave behind. For instance, Sardar had no idea what he was sitting on, the value of the basement. Sardar took a stab and guessed the builders might pay about a lakh if he moved out. Bhoosa! Two lakhs? Bichhu asked Ramji what kind of place he thought Sardar would get for two lakhs. Not even a tin shed. He asked Sardar to go out and take a look. Ranee brought up the subject of the wall coming up at the edge of the compound. The builders must have got a plan approved already. She asked what Sardar should do first. Bichhu listed the steps.

First, immediately, put up a board above the street entrance. Intercontinental Appliances and Service. Or something like that. Sounded good didn't it? IAS! The board must have the lines 'Established 1980' and 'Proprietor Shambhu Lal'. After that should they seek a meeting with the builders? Bichhu was emphatic that they should not. The builders must seek a meeting with Sardar. Next, they should lodge a complaint at the Police Station. The builders have started constructing a wall. They have dumped building material. These are encroachments. Illegal occupation of the compound space.

Ranee reminded Ramji that the builders had told them clearly the sale of the property was all pukka. Otherwise, how could they start work? Ah, that is what they all say. What did Ranee know about their methods? Why had there been no work for four months? Because it takes a lot to get the papers in order. A lot of patience. A lot of money. Meanwhile they collect advances from all those who want to book their flats. Cash down. No guarantee they'll get the flats. Cash down straight. That is why they must act fast, before the property is legally in the builder's name. Once they have the money, things will move in their favour. All eyes turned to Sardar. He had a question for Bichhu.

"Tell me, Bichhu, how old is this earth of ours?" Seeing a blank face he repeated, "How old is this earth?"

"How old? I don't know. Thousands of years old."

"Thousands? How many thousands?"

"I suppose...about eight or ten thousand years."

"Eight or ten thousand! That's what you learned by going to the Middle East."

"How does it matter? All I know is that Man arrived on this earth with a bang. His job is to make the most of it while he is here, to rule the earth. Each man must do that in his lifetime, and go out with a bang too! And we must act fast."

Bichhu was getting impatient now, but was cotrolled before his Mamaji, waiting for his response. Sardar spoke to Ramji instead. There was something wrong. He couldn't accept it, it was not natural. How could people go on spending more and more on things that give us less and less in return? Bichhu cut in.

"Are you going to be repairing buzzers and stoves till you die?"

"No two stoves are the same. No two irons, no two table fans. Each of them is an independent soul. Only a family doctor knows how to reach the soul. Not your five hundred rupee injectionwallahs."

"Mamaji, I don't understand this. We are talking business, you are talking Pooja-paat or vegetable gardening or some such thing. We are talking in lakhs, you are talking in soiled notes of tens and fives. We are talking about a service station. You are...sorry, mamaji, you are chained to this workbench."

Ranee moved to Sardar's side. She spoke firmly to Bichhu and Ramji. The work bench there...when Sardar sits down to work there, it's the only world he knows, the only world he cares to be in. Bichhu added quickly that Shambhumama, sardarmama, was simply the best mechanic in this part of the city. Maybe the best in the whole city. He might not know it himself, but everybody else knew it. If he chose to put his god given gift to proper use, the world around him would be willing to pay.

Sardar looked at Ranee and said, "I have to think about it." He asked Ramji and the nephew to make themselves at home and left the basement. Ramji started to follow Sardar. Bichhu held him back.

Ramji spoke to Ranee. They couldn't turn back now. Sardar and Ranee could take till next morning, but they had to go along. Bichhu pressed an envelope into Ranee's hand. A gift he had brought for them. Yes, it was money. They could treat it as an advance. There was fifty thousand there...useful for immediate expenses...A gesture of sincerity. An earnest deposit. They would take their leave. Ramji asked Ranee to speak to Sardar later, when his mind was clear.

"You know him better."

"His mind is clear now. It will not be any more clear later."

[This story has also been made into a play, titled Second Shift Muster. It was performed by the National Theatre in London in 1997, celebrating 50 years of independence in India and showcasing a collaborative project with Bangalore Little Theatre.]

The Crest

Big Chief they called him. He liked that. He demurred occasionally, not convincingly, asserting that he was simply doing his job, placed in the corner office by the powers above. In a business meeting they would simply say BC. It just happened that those were his initials as well. BC Sadashivaiah. The family name and his father's name were not easy to pronounce. So BC stuck. And who would ever call a man Sadashivaiah in an American multinational corporate office? He could easily have been Bob or Chid or Dash, but BC had the crispness of sound that suggested sharp business savvy. And it went with Big Chief.

In these times people are always interested in a company profile, so we can be done with that first before going ahead with the story of Big Chief.

PIL India Ltd., known simply as PIL, was the wholly owned Indian subsidiary of Pig Iron Lifestyles, a seventy five year old American Corporation. Originating in Pittsburgh as a family owned business trading in ironware it grew rapidly in the war years as a reliable supplier of steel components for a wide range of transportation equipment, including those in military operations. Many of the products found ready application on the domestic front in the post-war boom of home improvement gadgets and convenience products. In no time at all the Company found itself diversifying into foods, cosmetics and self-help healthcare. Most of it was through smart acquisition of businesses with established products who did not have the means to scale up. The hardware image of the Company quickly transformed to the Lifestyle image. It was not without some sadness that the old companies let go the big gadget brands – the Otter all-in-one blender, the ShipShape range of tools.

The brands remained vibrant in the marketplace, the buyers still loyal, but not knowing who made them.

PIL decided to concentrate on the Fast Moving Consumer Products line of business. Large volumes was the guiding strategy. They now had manufacturing facilities in twelve countries and marketing operations in over sixty countries. It was a matter of some pride for the company that in many poor countries where they did not have a presence their products were hot property in the smuggling trade. What would a mother not pay for a 4-pack of PIL's Acres brand baby food? Or the Petalips brand skin rejuvenator?

When Pig Iron Lifestyles came to India the Company chose to register as PIL, rather than the full American name. The Indian business partners had commissioned a reputed market research firm (also of American origin) to recce the marketplace and had found that the parent company's name would not go down well in India. Pig Iron was actually quite proud of its Pittsburgh origins and the humble ironmonger beginnings from where they had come a very long way indeed. The seasoned business house that the company was, the recommendation was readily adopted.

Hard work, dedication, enterprise and innovation were the core values of the Company, and it rewarded employees who displayed these values on the job. BC was certainly one of them, picked early to be put on a fast track.

That should do as company profile. We return to Big Chief.

BC was one of a select group of managers in the company who had been elevated to the cadre of Global Managers. It meant that their expertise was of value to other operations in other countries. Once every five years the company took up a massive Strategy Review & Planning exercise spread over an entire quarter, involving every business unit in every part of the world. It fed into a week-long apex event at headquarters in Pittsburgh, followed by a fling in the Bahamas, where the coveted corporate awards were announced. BC had received the much sought PIL baton twice. The length of leather had a beautiful dark finish that spelt class. At one end was a gold thimble tip. The crest at the other end was a gold crown with the company coat of arms engraved. The two batons were on display in the reception area of the company's India office. They were kept crossed in the glass case like two swords in an army commandant's office. There was every chance that BC would make the hat trick in the next gathering. That was just eighteen months away. Meeting targets and exceeding them was what every other manager at PIL did. BC had to do much more than that. He had to live up to his reputation as a trailblazer.

⌘ ⌘ ⌘ ⌘ ⌘

Big Chief was not very big made. In fact he was hardly seen in management team meetings, seated at on end with his head barely above the table top. Five feet nothing in his socks, his towering presence was felt nevertheless in the masterly conduct of meetings. And the implicit faith people had in his judgment. And the unqualified acceptance of his leadership. They say that people compensate for their deficiencies in some way or the other, even unknown to themselves. Some men with mediocrity written on their brows choose smart, articulate friends. Maybe it suits the smart-articulate person too in some way. Some plain looking women cultivate the friendship of good-lookers. We can expect some short men to pick tall men to call buddies. Or tall women for company to be seen in.

BC had people taller than himself all around him all the time. He did not pick them. They picked him. His wife was five inches taller than him. A more devoted spouse would be impossible to find anywhere. BC had the most talented and experienced managers in his team. They were roaring tigers in their operational territories. You saw mice in the management team meetings on Fridays.

BC's closeness to Pittsburgh gave him a stature of even greater awe in the India office. It also gave him a management style that came to be called Fast-n-Furious. Or simply Double-F. His war room exercise for market penetration was the stuff of legends. Nobody could get the energies of departments and functions to converge on a mission the way he did. Would you like to know how he won the last corporate baton? They could easily make a movie out of it.

The management team is assembled. The oval table is full. Around it are five comfortable chairs with the Divisional Heads seated. At one end is Big Chief. Only his head is seen, the jaw resting on the table edge. He speaks.

"All those in favour, say Yes and raise your hands, please. Only one hand to be raised, please, and it must be the right hand."

All five right hands are raised. This is the momentous start to one of the greatest marketing innovations in the company's history, one that simply had to be included as a case study in Harvard Business School.

Everybody knew that Vapos was unchallenged in the mentholated balms market. With a market share of over 90 percent it was the greatest contributor to the Indian company's bottom line year after year after year. Every housewife in every city and town had a jar of Vapos in her medicine cabinet. The advertising was predictably brilliant. The white coated physician in the clinic was seen asking the mother with the sniffing child, "Don't you keep Vapos at home?" The model playing the part of the housewife looked into the camera and got the exact combination of guilt as a non-performing mother and the innocent charm that said she would make up for it.

Tiny cottage industry units peddling the same mix of camphor, menthol and eucalyptus oil as grandmother recipes served only the grandmothers. Ah, but the company was not celebrating. There was no scope for growth, that six letter word that defined business success. Market research had ruled out further market penetration. And, horrors, the people who watched TV advertising were not producing children anymore. The 90-plus percent market share was now looking like an albatross.

BC changed all that. He changed that by changing the rules. "If we can't alter the demographics, we will get them to use more of it. Think volumes!"

In the first year the man in the white coat was showing the mother how to spread the balm from the throat to the whole chest. A year later he was showing her the benefits of turning the child over gently and spreading the balm on the back as well. "For faster, fuller relief." This was accompanied by the introduction of a larger pack that was called the Family Friend. (Both Double-F, incidentally.) Two years later the earnest mother's face was educating the viewer about the importance of keeping the feet warm when the child had a cold. The best way to do that was to rub Vapos generously on both feet up to the shins and to then cover up with a blanket.

In five years of the new marketing strategy the market share remained practically the same, but the volume of sales went up five-fold. In the year-end sales jamboree BC raised a toast to the team and added an aside, "Eat your heart out, grandma!"

What the Harvard case study omitted out of political correctness was the last thrust in BC's campaign. It was to extend the market horizons in the North-East. A chance observation by a sales executive had shown that there was a fair amount of Vapos smuggling across the border to both Bangladesh and China.

What they used it for was more interesting. Fingertip quantities of the balm put on the tongue and rolled about in the mouth before swallowing kept you warm – something they learned from their contacts this side of the border.

Demand far exceeded supply and only a small but steady smuggling trade flourished. All you needed to do was to increase the supply to this side of the border. The locals would take care of the rest. It was all legit. The market even grew...because it was addictive. BC admitted to his innermost circle that the business model for this campaign was inspired by the East India Company and the opium wars in China.

⁂ ⁂ ⁂ ⁂ ⁂

A person's rank and standing in a multinational corporation is seen in the rest rooms. The rest rooms all look the same, but the doors of Senior Executive rest rooms have locks. The keys are given, of course, to Senior Executives. A little higher up the echelon members of the Company Management Team have individual rest rooms with exclusive parking rights. In addition to the parking bays in the basement.

BC's rest room was rather special, approved by Pittsburgh. It had a shower cubicle, of course. It also had a mini-library on one side of the toilet seat and a draw-down writing board that BC could use when seated. The wall in front of the toilet seat was covered almost entirely by a monitor screen. The platinum hued acrylic top of the writing board slid back to reveal a slim keypad and mouse connected wirelessly to a processor that displayed inputs on the monitor on the front wall. It was no secret that BC spent a lot of time in the rest room. That is where his greatest ideas were born and incubated.

Onward! Forward! BC was appointed CEO of South Asia Region.

Upon his suggestion global R&D was now located in India. Product innovation was one of the mandates of R&D, overseen by BC. Corporate Intelligence identified Dr. Bishwanath Majumdar as a possible head of R&D at PIL. With a background in neurophysiology and biophysics Majumdar headed a project group in Chinar Labs that had a high reputation in research based product development. It was known that Majumdar was a top authority in studies of the Hunger Centre in the brain. Exactly what the project was in Chinar Labs was never known, a tightly guarded subject. BC's own investigations led to Dr. Majumdar winning hands down in the search process.

BC found that Majumdar had touched the glass ceiling at Chinar Labs. He was seen as a brilliant scientist and a doer, but not a leader and initiator. He would not go beyond project leadership at Chinar. BC snapped him up. And gave him the moniker Jomo to make him feel at home.

BC assembled his new team quickly. There was Bhogender Singh, Bobo, the maverick sales manager who carpet-bombed Gujarat with Aunt Katie's Ready-to-Serve American Apple Pie. Gajendra Pal Yadav was the brand manager whose paper products from elephant poo were coveted gifts to visiting dignitaries at Buckingham Palace. They called him Palloo. Jagga, from Jagganath of course, was the consumer behavior wizard. He had headed the award winning Chill-Fill Communications for Alpino Foods & Beverages. It had all of Kashmir Valley, Himachal and Uttarakhand stock eighteen flavours of ice cream and kulfi through the months of November to February. Last heard the Communication was replicated in Alaska when the company was bought over by a food and beverages American multinational. Big Chief remained BC, the only one known by his initials. Two more joined BC's top table team a month later, both women. One was for product reliability, drawn from a kitchen products company. The other, a social-anthropologist, was exclusively for feet-on-the-ground field studies. The last member of the team was Chips, the cybernetician who had been BC's right hand over twelve years. There was nothing about computer hardware and software and servers he did not know. The ever galloping rate of data mining needs was something BC knew instinctually, and Chips knew in configurations.

The countdown had begun for the first war room conference. Two entire days were spent in outfitting the space. It also had to be thoroughly sanitized, triple checked for bugs, sound leaks, radio wave leaks and hidden spy-cams. A double door entrance ensured zero interruption. A shredder-pulper was installed by the door so that not a square centimeter of paper left the room.

BC personally supervised the installation of the interlocked computer system in the war room, accompanied by Chips. He had seen long ago that managers became uncontrollably animated in a creative engagement. They use all available pieces of paper and draw diagrams on them, adding equations, flow charts, quotes from General Patton and Confucius, lyrics from pop music and dialogues from Sholay. In short they are school children on a picnic once again. You can also catch them glancing in the direction of the teacher every now and then, seeking approval.

"How about this one, sir?"

"Look at this, look at this!"

BC knew that the most creative outputs from the team were in the chemistry across ideas and not in the ideas themselves. No matter how brilliant each idea might be. He had Chips design and fabricate special swivel chairs, in the arms of which were docked freshly minted tablet-looking devices specially developed for the war room. Its toy-like appearance was, of course, deceptive. Chips called it a TabServe. Each of these devices had the storage and data mining capacity of a full bloom server in the basement. And what it was not capable of doing! The TabServes around the table were not only inter-faced wirelessly among themselves but also to a central console that processed the inputs on each tablet to seek out patterns across the ideas. The masterstroke algorithm achieved the conversion of every input in every form into a compatible language – squiggles, mathematical symbols, line drawings, even the voice exclamations, expletives and all. Out came a meta-analysis that told the group what they might possibly mean. That, in turn, led to another romp with renewed rigour and the excitement of a goal in view.

They call this iteration in the jargon. For BC it was just baking a cake. For the team it was limitless wine tasting. Waiting for a light at the end of the tunnel was not half as much fun as hurtling down the tunnel.

As in war rooms of the other kind, nobody had any sense of the time spent there, or the time of day outside. All watches were left behind, and there was no clock inside the room. All bio needs, both inputs and outputs, were met without fuss by automated means. It was never talked about.

Finally...the team saw BC raising his arms slowly heavenwards. His head followed. And then that famous grin on his face, the buck teeth fully revealed. All the chatter in the room ceased. All eyes turned to BC. Much like the rising sun, the figure at the end of the table gained size and volume steadily, revealing the shoulders, the chest and the torso. BC was standing on his chair. He had plucked out the tablet from its dock at his seat and was waving it to the whole team.

From the chair he conducted the finale of the orchestral piece, raising it to a grand crescendo.

"We have a Yin!" he exclaimed in his high pitched voice. "We have a Yin!" chorused the team in response.

"We have a Yang!" he exclaimed.

"We have a Yang!" chorused the team in response.

A dramatic pause. The team waited for BC to reveal to the wise men and women in the room the shape of the full pachyderm. Tablet in hand, BC climbed up, strutted to the centre of the oval table and delivered his proclamation.

"The Yin part of the Corporation will comprise four business units. They will be driven by the principal ingredient developed in R&D, code named Sparkler."

The team, now sober, thumped the table top and congratulated Jomo in unison with a very parliamentary "Hear hear". Sparkler was Jomo's breakthrough. He had successfully cracked the balance-restoring code in the autonomic nervous system. With the right chemical trigger it was possible to induce a process by which the human organism would continuously seek higher and higher levels of gratification. This would be seen in practically all kinds of consumption and stimulus-seeking behaviour. That would include food, of course, but many other highs as well – tobacco, alcohol, sex, extended to speed, adventure, aggression and vandalism. It was called threshold enhancement. Higher! Faster! Kinkier! The list of behavior channels appeared endless. The most exciting of these was in the potential for compulsive wasteful behavior and the vast increase in litter and garbage.

PIL had the formula for the chemical trigger safely deposited in an underground vault. It could be introduced into the human body through almost any intake carrier, from cookies to tomato ketchup.

BC continued. He announced that the four businesses together would push goods and services to meet all the consumption and hedonistic needs of the population...For what? Another dramatic pause. The team had to be shown.

"To systematically fuck up the environment". BC noted the aahs and the oohs. He smiled to let them know that their grasp was appreciated. He continued. "Ye are the rakes of the earth! And ye shall lead the way to fuck up the earth!" They thumped the table again as they chanted: "Rakes! Rakes! Rakes! Rakes!"

"Then...we have the Yang! It will be the other part of the business, made up of four other business units. They represent PIL's participation in the green economy. What do these four businesses have in common?" There were blank expressions, signaling a go-ahead to BC to give them the answer.

"Shit!" All our green businesses are about taking all kinds of shit and making it beautiful. We are the earthworms of this world." A tube light pause was followed by a roaring applause, then followed by the chant: "Earthworms! Earthworms! Earthworms!" BC tapped the table top with his custom-made platform heels.

"So...the Earthworms will come in with goods and services that sex up the environment." Another pause, another smile. He knew he had led the team to the final lap and had to now leave it to them to dash to the finish line. Immediately, on their own, the team regrouped into two huddles on two sides of the table, the Rakes and the Earthworms. They started to fine tune the strategic vision into a business plan, getting the gives and the takes right between the fucking-up and the sexing up. It was done soon enough. It would all begin with the massive campaign:

DO NOT SEGREGATE YOUR WASTE.

It would go on to show that the effort was a waste, that there is a better way, that it is all right to go ahead and consume more in the first place.

From two sides of the table the heads turned upward to Big Chief, still standing there, to seek his approval. He helped the team conclude.

"Satisfied that there is no guilt about consumption anymore the population will...?"

The team completed the sentence for BC. "Consume even more!! Fuck up the planet some more!"

"And then?"

"We clean up once more. Sex it up some more!"

BC was now strutting back and forth on the table, punctuating the key words of his pronouncement.

"In accordance...with our social responsibilities...and commitments...of corporate citizenship...we will have served... the needs of the community... as well as the needs of society ... Everybody...HAPPY!"

⁂ ⁂ ⁂ ⁂ ⁂

As everybody expected Big Chief was relocated to Pittsburgh very soon. They created the new position of CSO in the company for him with a global reach and responsibility. The company had never had a Chief Strategy Officer before.

All in Pittsburgh knew that it was only a matter of time that BC would be Chairman and CEO of Pig Iron Lifestyles.

Before leaving India BC had taken care of the cloud seeding to be nominated for a Padma award. A Padma Shri offer was discreetly upgraded to a Padma Bhushan by deft handling. It was announced within the year.

The South Asia office missed Big Chief, but they were nevertheless proud that it was their office that had given Pittsburgh a CSO. Visitors entering the office were greeted at the reception by a large colour portrait of BC in a gilded frame. Under the frame was the glass case which now had three batons with gold crests.

[This story has also been made into a short play. It is included in a set of sketches titled The Bottom Line.]

•••

The Peck

The flight was airborne at last. The three hour delay was the final blow. Why this day? And why this flight? Another hour and a half and she would be in Bangalore, although still over forty five kilometers from home. Another two hours and she would be there. Home. At last.

Shalini had accepted fully that she would miss the funeral the moment she got to know. It was a little after midnight. She realized that at two in the morning at home there would be many phone calls to be made. She should not be hogging the line more than really needed. He was gone. It was not entirely unexpected, but Appa was gone. She was among the first to be informed, there were other calls to be made. She thought she would make it easier for them by signing off herself. "I will call as soon as I have a booking. Please take care of Amma. Yes, I will call soon." There was a short silence from the other end that said they didn't know what to say. And finally the click and the dial tone that said it was all over.

Shalini got down to the job of finding a flight connection straight away. The internet search, the phone calls, the internet again, more calls. The holiday season had begun, she was informed, and there was simply no booking available till the day after. Would the lady be interested in a First Class ticket? Business Class? Shalini was convinced that death was an underground ally to airline companies with sagging sales curves. Yes, she would consider Business Class. Yes, she should be wait-listed. Yes, she would take the longer route if there was a chance to get her to Bangalore any quicker. Portland-JFK-Frankfurt-Mumbai-Bangalore was going to be nearly twenty four hours, but she would take it.

At every airport lounge, through all the flight announcements, Shalini's thoughts centred around the same question. Would she get home in time? She was thinking of Amma. She had seen this in so many funerals. The house is filled with a crowd of relatives from all parts of the country, helping out, chipping in, clearing up. Shalini would love to see them, although not under the happiest circumstances, but her thoughts were really not about arrivals. They were about departures. She could see it happening, they were departing, each at a chosen time, each in a different direction. It would be so much like the flight departures announced every other minute. They kept Shalini awake so she did not miss her own connection. They would keep Amma engaged for a while. And then, with a finality of purpose, there would descend the great emptiness.

⁂

"Why are we going through all this?" It was a question that came up again and again. Shalini voiced it openly. A few others mumbled agreement. But it was clear that The Family had taken charge. Appa might have displeased them now and then with his rationalist objections to all religious rituals, but he was a much loved elder in the community. Ritual reflexes, he called them, not without an admonishing tone. Or ritual ramblings. Or godforsaken rituals, if he was less patient with their insistence on self deception. They laughed, remembering that they loved him, but went ahead with the reflexes anyway. At other times they simply kept out of his way. Malavalli Narayana Rao Seshagiri Rao was not called Rao Bahadur for nothing. But now the conscientious dissenter was no more.

It was the considered opinion of The Family that once Appa's spirit had vacated the body, he had no say in the matter of last rites to be performed. The antyeshthi samskara for a Deshastha Brahmin could not be compromised, whether or not he subscribed to other samskaras in his lifetime. They knew, of course, that Appa had not. Shalini had wondered on the flight if she could be part of the last journey, accompanying the vacated body to the crematorium. She imagined a line of select members of the family, a few loved ones, a few really close friends, all in spotless white kurta-pyjamas, salwar-khameez, sarees, starched, quiet, dignified, paying their last respects as the bier was taken away into the inner room. It was not to be. Not because her return was too late anyway, but Appa's last journey was not to the crematorium run by the Municipal Corporation. It was to the cremation spot on the banks of a pond that was once a lake, where the truly devout cremated a body in the truly traditional way. No women allowed. Shalini had been informed by one of the dissenting mumblers who witnessed the cremation that it was solemn and awe inspiring, and even dignified in its own way. The small group waited till the skull burst open at the peak of cremation with the sound of a damp diwali cracker. They were then permitted to leave. The ashes were collected the next day.

Shalini reached home in time to see the pot of ashes placed in its designated corner. It was behaving itself. It was the very corner where Shalini was made to stand, not infrequently, not too long ago, when she had not behaved herself. Just in time. The next day the pot would be taken to Srirangapatna. They would be immersed at the Pashchim Vahini confluence of the Kaveri river. She could not see Appa, but she thought she was thankful she could see the ashes. There was some discussion among the mumblers whether they could join the elite squad going to Srirangapatna the next day. Before the decision could be pronounced Shalini announced she would rather stay back. She needed to get some sleep and get her bio-clock back in rhythm, she said. It was a wise decision, The Family said.

She had really taken after Appa. That is what she was told as god's truth in childhood. She had heard it echoed from every branch of the family tree ever since. Especially her scientific bent of mind, they said. Shalini was not sure what that was supposed to mean. She imagined it had something to do with her choosing Art History as the course for her Masters in the US, with Comparative Religion as the elective. Who cared if nobody understood why she took subjects with such strange sounding names. Appa was happy. She was doing what she wanted to do. He was convinced that you could do well in Comparative Religion as a rationalist.

Shalini had often wondered if Appa would accept her as a rationalist. She had a marble Ganesha in the living room of the home in Portland. She was not sure why it was there, and why she did pooja on Ganesha Chaturti day. Perhaps it was forgivable in Portland. There would be a stream of visitors after six in the evening. Serving prasad was mandatory, a mix of Kannadiga and Maharashtrian recipes, along with good Californian wine.

⁂ ⁂ ⁂ ⁂ ⁂

Abdul always switched off his mobile phone at namaz. In a hurry that morning he had forgotten. Fortunately it was just an SMS beep . He put the phone off, but not without noting that the message was from his old friend, Achar. They had been friends since their Government Primary School days. He was called Chari then. After SSLC they had gone their separate ways, but had remained friends. Garudachar was an Upper Division Clerk in a Railway department. He was eligible for promotion as a Grade 3 Supervisor, but he had learned to be patient. Abdul had drifted, trying his hand at renting bicycles, car and motorbike mechanics, timber contracts at bamboo bazaar, a newspaper agency and even a salaried job as Office Manager in a bus tours company. The old school did not teach them great maths or great cricket, but they learned about responsibility and hard work and doing your best. And not worrying too much about tomorrow. They also learned what great friendship was all about. There were others in the old gang, Cheenu, Anto, Saboo and Zafar. They would get together once in a while, at a wedding or a festival, especially if there was going to be a biriyani spread. It was only when Abdul got married that Chari discovered his full name was Abdul-Haq, which meant the servant of truth.

Abdul and Chari stayed in touch more regularly. In recent times it was mostly by mobile phone, often just an SMS exchange, but it was sufficient. When they did meet it was usually a long ride for a bite at a dhaba on the highway. Sometimes it was on Abdul's Hero Honda, other times on hamara Bajaj that Achar had got with a loan soon after his confirmation at the Railway office. Sometimes they met at Abdul's chabutra, where he raised pigeons. It was here that Achar learned that rearing birds and training them was a science in itself. Abdul had explained how he would clip the bird's wings in the training period to keep it grounded, and allow them to grow again later. A pigeon can learn to do all kinds of things. They say that a famous psychologist in America even trained a pair of pigeons to play ping pong. The pigeons reared for endurance flying were different. They were generally dark and had to be kept grounded longer and given a special diet of mixed pulses.

"Monday 7 am" the SMS had said. "Ok" Abdul had replied. As he walked back to the motorbike, shiny and bright after its morning bath, Abdul called Achar and asked how his family was. Yes, he got the SMS. No, he would not forget, it would be done. Why was Achar so edgy? So many questions. He wanted to know if Abdul would be there himself on Monday morning, or would he send his son? Abdul said he would tell him if he answered his own questions first. After all, he had called. How was Bhabhiji? All thik thak at home? All right, he would be there himself if Chari wished. But what was special? Whose tenth day ceremony was it?

"Appaji Rao", replied Achar, softly

"Rao Bahadur?"

"The same."

"God rest his soul in peace! When did he... ?"

"Exactly. We must do everything we can to make sure his soul rests in peace. And that's where you come in."

"Certainly, certainly."

Achar, like some other men in his family, was also a priest. It topped up his income at the Railway office just enough to afford a few things for the family. He was able to send his son and daughter to a private school where they could study English. Achar had learned to be a priest by being an apprentice to his father, the venerable Narasimhachar, who was a full time priest in his time. Most homes seeking Achar's services were Brahmin. Not all were as orthodox as those that came to his father. They were knowledgeable and uncompromising in those days, and his father gained immense satisfaction from meeting their demands. Things were different now. It came as a surprise that Appaji Rao's family wished to have a full and proper tenth day ceremony to persuade his restless spirit to retire peacefully in the ancestral pitraloka. Achar knew that Appaji's spirit would be in a state of great turmoil from knowledge of the unchecked string of rituals after it left his body. It had to be calmed. It could not be left to suffer, forever a dissatisfied preta.

Abdul's family had taken care of the shamiana services at all of the ceremonies from Narasimhachar's time. Abdul himself would be present to make sure everything was set up exactly as required. Over the years he had learned to read on the faces of the families what the set up should be. From mundan ceremonies to upanayanams, from marriages to deaths, from ten guests to a thousand, every occasion had its special needs, and every family a character of its own. It didn't seem to matter at all that his name was Abdul-Haq, not in the old days. Now, to be on the safe side, he had chosen the name Aishwarya Shamiana Services. He even threw in the catering on some occasions, especially at weddings. Nobody would ever guess that the crisp masala vade came from Abdul's kitchen. Others more particular would have a Brahmin caterer, who often relied on Abdul for the banana leaves.

Abdul knew a thing or two about Hindu samskaras. The antyeshti last rite for Appaji Rao's soul was going to get his undivided attention.

⁂

It was a prolonged debate, cordial and civil, but with an unmistakable undercurrent. The flow was punctuated at the right moments by Shalini's quotes from the sutras and smritis, appropriately endorsed in mumbles. Not unexpectedly, a compromise formula was found for the remaining last rite.

First and foremost, the actual ceremony would be undertaken only by the designated male members of the family. This would be at the spot chosen by the family three generations ago, as the entire lineage of male ancestors had to recognize the ceremony and welcome the soul of Appa into their midst. The pinda would be kept for the visiting crow at the same flat stretch of rock next to the ruins of the old fort wall. Achar explained that three other pinda ceremonies were expected on Monday morning. He had arranged for an exclusive small shamiana for the family at about fifty meters from the stone where the pinda was to be kept. They would watch from there.

Secondly, the female members of the family wishing to attend the ceremony would only be silent witnesses, seated at a further distance behind, perhaps in the shade of the shrine on the mound. A second shamiana might be set up there, if needed.

Finally, Amma would not be present for any part of the pinda ceremony. She would wait at the temple till the end, when she would be called upon to break her bangles and enter her new station.

⁂ ⁂ ⁂ ⁂ ⁂

Crows. Shalini decided to find out more about them that night. In the privacy of Appa's study, which had been outfitted with a mattress just for her, she first did her mails, mostly single sentences, acknowledging with thanks the condolences offered. She then switched to her search.

The Corvidae family includes a large group of birds besides crows and the closely resembling ravens. Do all these birds have something in common? They are described as "curious, intelligent, noisy, outrageous, and social". The ratio of a crow's brain to its total mass is far ahead of all other birds. It is similar to that of mammals, including primates. Crows have pronounced forebrains, the part responsible for learning and memory. They have a strong memory for human faces and voices. Crows can count to six, perhaps eight. They exercise restraint in matters of consumption, saving for the future and lean times. Crows take the trouble to hide a large quantity of food before beginning to eat. Far from being "ravenous", they can be very choosy about what they will eat, and when.

How did it come to be that this much despised bird became so very important for the rite of pindadana? The crow appears as the messenger of Yama. The prayer seeking its indulgence, begging it to accept the pinda offering, is meant to satisfy the hunger of the departed spirit that is wandering, seeking the abode of Yama.

Within minutes Shalini was falling asleep at the laptop. She would continue the search the next day. Some field investigations appeared in order.

⌘ ⌘ ⌘ ⌘ ⌘

Monday morning. The house was abuzz by five, the strong aroma of coffee wafting through the rooms. Shalini entered the living room bathed and ready. The garland on Appa's portrait had already been changed. Did she spot a hitherto unnoticed grin at the corner of his lips? He seemed to have just said to her: "Well, get on with it!"

Who would perform the ceremony? Appa had no son, so Puttanna, his younger brother, had performed the last rites at the cremation. But he had left for Kolkata soon after. Achar offered to do the needful on behalf of the family. He would gladly do so, and the family gladly accepted. Would women be allowed? Why not, asserted Achar. Shalini was the only taker. Achar explained that the spot of the actual ceremony would have only him. It would be hot and probably dusty. A small shamiana was being erected for family members nearby. There were to be four of them.

The ceremony had commenced by the time the family members got there. Abdul took his leave, but not before exchanging short prayers with Achar that all may go well. Achar had commenced the preliminaries. He was seated about fifty meters from the area where families placed the pinda offerings. As decided, the shamiana for the family was another ten meters behind. The view was solemn, but resembled a picnic site.

The pinda offering was ready. As prescribed it was cooked rice mixed with ghee and black til seeds. A dash of fresh jaggery was added, a weakness of Appa. It was all shaped by hand the size of billiard balls. The invocation of ancestors in the Bharadwaja gotra was followed by the appeal to proceed with the final rite. Finally, it was time for the offering. Achar began the chant on behalf of the family: "May this pinda wait upon the preta separated from the body of Seshagiri Rao, son of Narayana Rao, son of Prahlada Rao of Bharadwaja gotra..." It ended with the fervent wish of the family that the hunger and thirst of the spirit may be appeased, and its restlessness put at ease. Achar walked down and placed the pinda on a banana leaf on the flat rock meant for it. Achar then advised the two men to declare that they would fulfill the last wishes of the departing soul.

They looked up at the sky. There was not a crow in sight. In fact, there were no birds of any kind. Achar explained that the microwave towers for cell phones were responsible for the disappearance of birds. The men were nervous. Achar suggested that they close their eyes and concentrate on Appa, especially what he might wish from those present. Could a woman participant do that too, Shalini wondered. She was not going to ask. She closed her eyes anyway.

How silly, she thought, doing this to please Appa, but doing exactly what Appa would disapprove. She struggled with this a few moments and then realized that she was not doing what she set out to do, which was to think of Appa's wishes. Silly. She decided to wake up. As she opened her eyes, she saw he was there already.

It was a rather large, well endowed bird, strutting from behind the wall ruins, pausing, surveying the scene, strutting again, pausing again. He carried himself like a Sergeant Major. The men whispered to Shalini. He looked like Appaji Rao Bahadur! Shalini hushed them, but did not disagree. Achar motioned to the men to remain absolutely still. The bird took its time stepping up to the pinda.

He seemed to sense the anxiety in the three men seated in the distance, enjoying the power he had over them. He bent down over the rice ball, paused, straightened up, and turned his head to a side, as if to say he had seen better. A soft gasp from the men. A reassuring wave from Achar. He whispered to them again, asking them to think of any unfulfilled wishes of Appa.

How would they know? Shalini closed her eyes again and remembered her offer to catalogue all of Appa's negatives from a lifetime of black and white photography. When she opened her eyes the Sergeant Major was looking straight once again, but not bending down to eat. She closed her eyes once more. In a flash came images of the letter Appa had written her six months ago. He had known that time was running out. Uppermost in Appa's mind for some time was the question of Amma's care after he had gone. Of course she would be there, she had assured him. That was not enough, he had replied. She had to live in dignity. Shalini knew what that meant. It was The Family. She was determined to take the necessary steps at the earliest. As a matter of fact, just last evening she had got all the older women of the household to agree that Amma might break her bangles for the sake of form, but she would retain her bindi and all her jewellery, and wear them with pride whenever she wanted to.

When she opened her eyes the Sergeant Major had turned reasonable. He took a peck at the pinda and straightened up. He was clearly testing the nerves of the men seated there. Another peck, another stare. Then came a proper bite, followed by a muted grunt that seemed to say thank you. He then proceeded to complete the job with a flourish. The flourish, the flourish, the cousins exclaimed, so like Appaji.

In the evening, with the tiffin tucked away, the family was in a distinctly relaxed mood. Amma joined the group. She was wearing a saree Shalini recognized immediately. Appa had given it to her on his return from Benaras. Somebody sang a bhajan. Another tried a Saigal piece Appa loved. Other Appa favourites were recalled, the songs, the pictures, the jokes, the anecdotes and, of course, his admonitions. It was then time to talk about the Vaikunta Samaradhne, and the lunch menu, with Appa's favourite dishes. Whatever the omissions, the chiroti simply had to be included.

At about the same time Achar and Abdul were sharing a plate of onion pakodas over chai at the dhaba. Achar was immensely grateful to Abdul for his services that morning. Nothing to it, he was just doing his bit, Abdul said. Everything thik thak in the end. Achar was worried about the future of the samskara.

"The crow not turning up is a serious problem for some."

"It can only get worse."

"Rao Bahadur's family is very special. I don't know what I would have done without you."

"Always at your service."

"To think that you played a part in resting a soul in peace..."

"Nobody need know."

The break in the conversation, the silence, the whirr of the chai being sipped. They exchanged smiles and ordered another round of pakoda. Achar wanted to continue.

"How long will you go on with this?" asked Achar.

"As long as you ask me to."

"And if I can't go on myself anymore?"

"As long as there are restless spirits that need peace."

"And your... crows?

"All part of the service. The demand is increasing. I will have to put more of them on the job."

Achar asked what would happen if somebody found out. Abdul stared hard at the saucer of chai under his nose. He glanced up at Achar. He asked Achar to think about the last rite he had performed so many times. What was it really all about? Was it not about peace? Anything that helps to keep peace in the family is all right. If the departed soul is happy, there is peace in the family.

[Death rituals can be tragically funny. A bunch of sketches was developed for the stage titled Exit Laughing. The set includes the idea in this short story that the dead have no say in the rituals that follow. In another short play by Rabindranath Tagore we see that the nearly departed has no say even when alive.]

The Piggery

When I took a break from studies it was simply that, a break. I had got a degree, so that the family could say their son was a graduate. In the last semester of my three years in college I was not sure what it meant. To be a graduate. Fifteen years on, I still don't know.

Two years after I left home I found myself holding an office in the college Students Union. The Princy had a rare sense of humour. He congratulated the student audience at the inaugural function on their unity, their democratic sense and their purposeful endeavours. But one wave of his magic wand, and the Executive Committee was disbanded. That was when the Students Union sought more information about the appointment of a new mess contractor who, only incidentally, resembled Princy's wife in physical appearance and spoke the same dialect from the same district. It was only a matter of minor detail that the police were brought in the next day, and divided we fell. At least I did, with four stitches on my head, a couple of broken ribs.

I spent most of my spare time in college at the Rural Extension Centre. It was a small group and we had a number of things to do in our twice-weekly trips to the nearby village – the dispensary, the demonstration plot of land, the adult literacy class, games with the children, and so on. Right from the start I had felt uneasy about our understanding of things. There was so little we knew about the lives of these poor people and so much that we were assuming. I found it difficult to believe what the Centre would have me, the villagers themselves and all else to believe, that they were poor because they were not making the required effort. I set myself a private research task to understand this better. In no time all, with no prior motive, this private research had turned into an extended study of quite another character. I began to see things my senses had not quite been prepared for. In an informal talk at the Centre I presented my analysis of the variety of effort that goes into keeping the rural poor in continued poverty. The next week the Rural Extension Centre had lost one member.

It was getting increasingly clear. I was going to take a break after I was done with the degree. I applied for an internship with an NGO of some repute. It was called People First. The full name was People For Integrated Rural and Social Transformation. A part of their success came from the support they received from a UK based international agency. As the internship was nearing its end they offered me a project staff position. I accepted without a second thought. People First had chosen an area near the old Kolar Gold Fields for a new project. Various earlier projects there by others had folded up for one reason or the other. The failure of the past was in fact one of the reasons People First chose to work there. They had a Development Model to offer. And they had a Plan.

⌘ ⌘ ⌘ ⌘ ⌘

Look up Kolar Gold Fields. It does not matter which search engine you choose, you will find many romantic accounts of the golden era of the mines. The names of many Englishmen will keep popping up. You are not likely to find anything about the wretched poverty there since the mines shut down.

Abrampalyam is a slum in Macphersonpet, in the vicinity of Kolar Gold Fields. It had about 300 families of which 91percent were Christians, and the rest Hindus. Of the Christians, over 90 percent were Catholics. I was learning. These distinctions and denominations were central to their lives. A majority of men did not work. Instead they resorted to petty thieving at night and idling during the day. Most families were engaged in distilling illicit liquor, a livelihood managed almost entirely by the womenfolk. Some additional income came from the sale of scrap metal, fixtures and brass fittings stolen through night patrols. There was also the gold dust panned from the earth and illegally carried away from the mining areas. The community was forced to accept whatever the pawn broker or goldsmith offered for the powdery substance submitted.

This slum had a long history of church and social work organisations visiting it and dispensing charity. One such Catholic organization, embarked on a grand employment generation scheme. They chose a group of ten women, all Catholics, consisting mainly of widows or women with invalid husbands, to whom they distributed cows. The cows had a foreign pedigree. A nun who worked for this organisation was put in charge. She felt that the whole community had to be involved, but nobody listened to her. Amelioration was a key word. It was expected that a grant of this kind would ameliorate their lot. The Rotary Club pitched in with a contribution. There was a photo-shoot of the cheque handing ceremony and it received prominent coverage in their Newsletter.

Within a span of two months, some had sold the cows, others pawned them or killed them for meat. On enquiring into the matter the women had a ready explanation. They complained that the cows had been thrust upon them, that they were old and not really the milch cows as proclaimed. Feeding and looking after these foreign animals was another story. It cost the earth. The families never spent a fraction of that on their own sustenance In short, it was an unprofitable venture. The nun who was in charge of their project had to leave Macphersonpet. She did away with the customary church practice and invited the pastor of the local Protestant church to take over the project.

After she left the community approached the pastor for his assistance in initiating a new employment scheme.

The pastor arranged for a series of lectures on animal husbandry, which were delivered jointly by the Block Development Officer, the project officer of Bangarapet, and others. Since the group had experience in raising country pigs, they chose piggery for the new employment project. The people themselves found out what they were entitled to according to the Government scheme. Each person could be given two sows and one boar. But the pastor's group took the position that employment should be created on a collective basis. The key phrase now was Target Group. A Cooperative had to be framed of the target group. Four or five widows formed the Cooperative and gave it a nice sounding Tamil name that could loosely be translated as "We go on". They did not seek legal registration for the Cooperative, but the members affiliated themselves to an Association of non-organized labour in the area.

There was a technical snag. The Government scheme had a provision for pigs to be given to individual beneficiaries. The officials did not know how to deal with a Cooperative. They had to be first convinced of the viability of collective effort. The members of the Cooperative themselves secured the certificates which made them eligible for the scheme and obtained the pigs collectively, standing guarantee for each other. The government office was impressed.

Next, the pastor helped the group prepare a representation to the municipality for a piece of land for the piggery project. They had to persist with their appeal for about eight months. They paid collective visits to the official concerned. The persistence paid off. The size of the group made an impact on the officials concerned. The local MLA said they could not afford to neglect such a large group. The group members also learned to assert themselves in dealing with government agencies.

The Cooperative finally obtained one acre of land near Abrampalyam. The municipality awarded them the land on condition that the project had to come up there within two years. About seven months passed before they could start construction of the building. The group agreed to give its free labour for the construction of the shed for rearing pigs. One person was sent for a month's training in pig rearing to Vellore. He would train the others on his return. The entire group went for a day to Hesaraghatta farm to learn about costing and management of a piggery, including fodder, housing and health care.

Around this time the pastor left Abrampalyam to take up a posting in another parish. The new pastor was not in favour of any direct involvement of the church in the Cooperative. He would attend meetings only if invited. The key phrase he used often was Self Reliance. He discouraged meetings of the Cooperative in the church premises.

It was not long before the pigs went the way of the cows. They were sold off or eaten. The women blamed the men. The men blamed the Protestant church. The church blamed the Catholic mentality. The municipality sent a reminder about having visible results from the project site.

It was about this time that People First appeared on the scene. A preliminary survey for base data had shown great potential, especially in view of a Cooperative already being there. The pastor offered to help in any way he could, as long as it did not call for any direct involvement of the church.

⌘ ⌘ ⌘ ⌘ ⌘

People First was bringing in their tried and tested twin-pronged development intervention model. The first prong was Alternative Technology for income and sustainable livelihood.

(Also shown as Appropriate Technology sometimes.) The second prong was Participatory Rural Appraisal. PRA was a hot new import.

Deep community participation in assessment and decision making was meant to increase ownership of enterprises, lead to greater involvement and, more important, become the means to non-formal education.

It had been developed in the UK and the international agency supporting People First was promoting it vigorously. What that meant was assured project funds. I was chosen to do the ground preparation at Abrampalyam. It was my first assignment with independent charge. I had already been sent to a PRA course in Bangalore and had received a certificate. I went through the PRA guidelines several times before my first meeting with the community. I even memorized the manual.

The first meeting. It was an all-woman gathering, of course. The main objective was getting to know each other. I took particular care not to mention the piggery project. They had to talk about it by themselves, if and when they wished. They did. The gist was that the project still existed, but needed much effort to be revived. We could look at it in some detail later, I said casually. Perhaps they could show me what was left of it. Meanwhile, it would help if I knew what sources of income the community had. There was the arrack, of course. The women were more than ready to show me how it was distilled, if I was interested.

I was not particularly interested, but went along. I found it very interesting indeed when I saw it. Even fascinating, I must admit. I made sketches, I took measurements, I timed the processes. Three large earthen pots kept one on top of another is the entire distillery. It is a pretty sight in itself. The bottom pot is stood on a wood fired chulha. It contains the basic brew, which is the fermented liquid from any combination of sugar-rich biomass. No different from wine making using fruits. Over-ripe bananas are the most cost-effective. The second pot has holes at the bottom, with large pebbles sitting loosely on the holes. An aluminium dish is kept on the pebbles inside the second pot. The vapours from the lower pot rise and flow past the pebbles in the second pot and hit the bottom of the third pot, kept on top. The third pot has cold water inside. Aha, the vapours are cooled by the third pot. They condense into a liquid and drop into the aluminium dish. Pure arrack! The basic brew for this process is prepared in individual homes, a sort of cottage industry. It is prepared in large plastic drum-like containers. The mouths of the drums are covered by two layers of muslin cloth. The cover allows the bubbling carbon dioxide to get out, and prevents the tiny fruit flies and other insects from getting in. The brew has little value in itself. The drums are marked in chalk to show the starting date for the brew. It takes anything from twenty five to thirty two days for the brew to be ready for distilling. A dash of metabisulphite yeast aids the fermentation and release of alcohol into the juice. The yeast is picked up from a bakery in Bangalore Cantonment by whoever happens to go there. The bakery also made port wine for its old-timer customers.

The project objective of People First was pragmatic and down to earth. The investments already made in the piggery needed to be rejigged into a viable enterprise. There were two main requirements. Upgradation in technology for meat processing, and innovations in distribution and marketing to reach consumers beyond Kolar District. Through the participatory process adopted the community would have ownership of the project. They would be aided to achieve the enterprise goals. The PRA manual laid out the process and the steps to be followed.

⌘ ⌘ ⌘ ⌘ ⌘

The women sent a message that they had completed their in-depth Appraisal and were ready for a discussion of the project plan with our staff. It would be at least a half-day workshop. My Programme Manager came in from Bangalore for the workshop. Two other management staff from People First accompanied him.

The meeting was held in the Piggery Cooperative premises. The temporary shed had been cleaned and spruced up. Chairs and tables had been hired. Tea and snacks were arranged for the kick off. At the centre of the shed was spread a large sheet of white flex. There was seating on the floor all around it, a few chairs for those who preferred to sit on them. The white flex had a prominent window drawn on it. It was a large square divided into four equal-sized smaller squares. On all four sides were pebbles of different colours and sizes. There were white board marker pens, red and green.

The women began by thanking People First profusely for what they had learned from us, and reiterating how important it was in shaping their lives. They were now ready to share their three-year plan with us. They had a project that was fool-proof. The SWOT analysis which they had learned from us had convinced them that it was the best thing they could do. Pointing to the grid on the white flex they said they would share their analysis with us straight away.

One woman took out a clay model of a simple hut and placed it at the top of a column to show that it represented the Internal Environment of the Cooperative and Abrampalyam. Another woman took out a model of Vidhana Soudha in Bangalore. Keeping it at the top of the second column she said it represented the External Environment. All the women then took out their gold earrings and kept them in a pile to say that they were the assets and things to be proud of. The pebbles were the wide variety of impediments and obstacles that came in their way. They took turns talking as the gold earrings and pebbles started filling up the four boxes on the flex sheet.

They arrived at the conclusion. The Cooperative wished to return to making arrack. They agreed with us completely on the two-pronged approach. They saw two main requirements that would be their programme thrusts as well. The first was technology improvements for scaling up production. The second was innovations in marketing to reach consumers beyond Kolar District.

The second thrust included quality assurance and branding to create a favourable image of arrack, overcoming the negative image of the drink in the public mind. The Cooperative was confident they could do it.

My Programme Manager was not quite prepared for this. He stared at the white flex in silence. When he realized that the group was waiting for him to say something, he said what he was trained to do: "It depends..." It meant it was not what he would approve. The group turned to me. I had to admit that the group had done a very good job of the SWOT, covering all the relevant points in the four boxes before us. The sheer business logic had also shown the superiority of the arrack project over the piggery project.

It was time for lunch. And time for some cool reflection. The Programme Manager drew me aside and asked me if the group had ever discussed the moral dimensions of going into the arrack business. I reported faithfully that the community had indeed discussed it in some detail. They had asked how shops along the highway sold bottled liquor with colourful labels openly. More cogent was their mission statement of a market presence giving their arrack the status of cashew feny in Goa. It was their considered decision that they should not be ashamed any more to run a legitimate business.

The Manager asked if I had thought about my future career. I said I would have to think about it some time.

[Participatory Rural Appraisal (PRA) was a widely used method in community organization programmes that led to Self Help Groups. It was developed to great procedural detail. Not surprisingly, participation as a technique tended to become more important than participation as a value.]

The Pilot

There was no hangover from the New Year eve party. The barking dogs on the street below and the chatter of the crows just outside the window were surprisingly tolerable, not the jack hammer drilling into the head as on earlier New Year mornings. The barking actually had a lulling effect on the half-awake Jayesh, extending his sleep by at least half an hour. The stillness after that made Jayesh wake up with a start. In less than ten minutes he had washed, showered, changed and was at his breakfast of two bananas and black tea. The five other members of the Campaign Scouts team arrived together and joined Jayesh. All six team members were in spotless white T-shirts over freshly laundered but fading indigo jeans. Sneakers had given way to gliders, all of them pale grey. They carried bandanas that would display the party emblem boldly when tied on the head. That would be when they stepped outside. They sipped their tea in silence. Jayesh broke the silence to signal that they were ready to leave. "Remember this at all times. We must get straight to the point. A bold statement. No wishy-washy prefacing, no pussy-footing, no beating about the bush." They synchronized their watches and closed in for a quiet huddle. They stepped out at exactly 8.10 am. The bandanas were on.

The team was ready to test the campaign platform at the very first pilot community gathering. Subbu-sir had picked five community sites for the pilots in different parts of the city. They had all to be done within half a day, before word of mouth exchanges and media reports influenced opinions. The recordings would be sent for examination to the Strategic Analysis Team for a verdict on the campaign plan. SAT, as they were called. The first target community was the lower middle class colony of tenements at the edge of JP Nagar.

The planned ground work had been done by the party's Volunteers Corps, popularly called the Sappers. There was nothing the Sappers did not know about softening up the area for an onslaught. A mid-sized gathering of about eight hundred was to be assembled in the playground of Shastriya College. The South side of the playground was used for both football and hockey. There was space for cricket at the centre and volleyball and basketball courts in one corner. Shastriya College enjoyed the reputation of being community-friendly, allowing the playground for a whole lot of civic events. People came too, simply because it was being held at Shastriya. It was the most appropriate location for the pilot test. Equally important was the fact that holding a public gathering there did not require formal police permission.

⌘ ⌘ ⌘ ⌘ ⌘

Krishnan was curled up inside his razai, the vague sense of a dream floating over his head. It was a ride through a desert on the pillion of Jayesh Uncle's motorbike. He was called by Krish by Jayesh. Nobody else was allowed to call him that. His mother called him Kittu.

He was on Jayesh Uncle's motorbike now. They swerved, they pitched, they tossed, the engine snorting like a bull in rage, roaring back to power for short stretches and challenged by yet another sand dune. They never stopped, they never fell off.

The dream did not say where they were going, where they started from. They just went on. It felt like a frontier was being approached, a frontier that had to be crossed for some powerful reason that only he and Jayesh Uncle knew. It was there at the back of Krish's mind, but never clearly laid out in the dream.

Every time he tried to recall the noble quest the dream would fade out and the screen would go blank. Krishnan would turn, drawing up the quilt, and the dream would come on again from the start, like a video strip in loop. The same dunes, the swerving, the pitching, the engine roaring.

One little corner of Krish's mind was asking if it could step in and bring the story to a close. Wasn't it obvious? It was the movie Jayesh Uncle had taken Krish to see on New Year eve. It was a desert jeep ride in the movie. It was a chase. There were four of them in the jeep. The villains had a head start, but everybody knew that the jeep would catch up with them and there would be a fight to the finish. The finish. The little corner was vetoed out. The loop was replayed once more. It had to be the motorbike ride and nothing else. Maybe this time he would get at least a glimpse of the climax. What was it that awaited them at the end of the desert?

Jayesh Uncle had dropped Krish home after the movie and had gone on to meet his friends for their own New Year eve party. It was in a farm house outside the city. Krishnan had dinner followed by a mandatory family viewing of a TV serial. Krishnan was upstairs a minute after the episode ended, in bed, inside the razai. He was asleep in less than five minutes.

⌘ ⌘ ⌘ ⌘ ⌘

Jayesh's team entered the playground at exactly the time given. They could see that the Logistics team had set up everything as given in the plan document. There was a long table for registrations next to the arched entrance to the main building. It had, among other things, a lucky dip basket with small gifts for participants, an array of six laptops behind placards that had the letters of the alphabet distributed across them.

There was a stationery counter from where they picked up a note book with an attractive pen in a plastic folder. From the registration tables people could go directly to the refreshments area, just behind. At the centre of the playground was the area for the opener meeting, with a high bandstand like stage set up with audio equipment. The space in front of the stage was for a standing audience only. All around the meeting area were two concentric circles of meeting tables for small groups of ten to twelve each. Across the ground from the registration tables was the Process Console, raised about twenty feet above the ground to provide a panoramic view of the entire playground and all the tables. Jayesh and the team saw that Subbu-sir was already up there.

Jayesh's team had allowed for a Bangalore Standard Time cushion of half an hour after 9.30 am, the time given for the event to actually start. The audio would be switched on exactly at the appointed time. The band with the two singers took the stage as soon as the refreshments had been set up. They would sing all time favourite duets from films. It would also serve as a reminder to all within a radius of 300 meters that they were expected there. It wasn't needed. The attendance was surprisingly good. And punctual. The number had crossed seven hundred by 9.45 am.

The registration touched 800 at 9.50 and was promptly closed. A signal was sent to the Process Console. Latecomers were turned away politely, but not without a tot of hot chai. They were allowed to watch the proceedings from the entrance, but not allowed in for the rest of the event.

The six-member team led by Jayesh ascended the steps of the stage, timing it with the end of a song. They had worn their head-set microphones and switched them on. Jayesh led the clapping, which was followed by a roar of applause from all the participants gathered around the stage. The monitor at the edge of the stage flashed an alert and the team took its place in an arc facing the audience, also in an arc around the stage. The monitor flashed a thumbs up sign. They were on.

The monitor would now be on prompt mode, ensuring the team covered the six essential points before the gathering was guided to the tables for the second part of the event, the substantial part.

Jayesh's team greeted the gathering in unison, palms pressed together: "Namaskara!" There were eight hundred full throated responses. It was clearly a good beginning. Jayesh's team had learned at the very first camp that the secret to political mobilization was audience participation in voice and body. Cheers, jeers, slogans, chants, rants, anything, but with raised voices and with all joining in. A quick reinforcer was in order. The team stepped forward and repeated the greeting, just a bit louder, more cheery. "Namaskara!", replied the audience. The monitor flashed the first prompt:

RIGHTS.

The team raised their arms, fists clenched and chanted together. "For us! By us!"

The predicted response followed. The team repeated the chant for a reinforcer. The reinforcing response followed. It was done three times. Nobody in SAT had explained why some things had to be done three times. It was simply to be done. The crowd seemed to expect it too. The monitor flashed the next prompt:

HOW.

It was agreed that Jayesh would fire the first salvo. He stepped forward, the rest of the team playing the chorus behind him.

"The food that you eat – where does it come from? You earned it by your hard work!"

A pause.

"The clothes you are wearing – where did they come from? Your hard work! The rent you are paying for a roof over your head – where did it come from? Your hard work!"

A slightly longer pause this time. Where was this heading? At this point Jayesh raised his voice and taunted the crowd.

"The government you have to rule over you – how did you get them there? What have you done to get the government you really want? Have you worked hard enough for that?"

The chorus behind Jayesh added the answer: "THIS is what we are here to discuss today! This is YOUR morning. We will not give you a lecture. We want YOU to think about how YOU may get a government YOU really want."

Jayesh added, "… And we have made arrangements for you to discuss this important question freely and openly."

He explained that the team would take just a few minutes more at the stage. After that the entire gathering would be seated in small discussion groups at the tables specially arranged all around. He asked for the crowd's permission to take those few extra minutes. Nobody had ever taken the crowd's permission for anything before. There was a lusty "Yes!" in response.

The monitor flashed:

POSE FIRST QUESTION.

It was time for a change of voice. A second member of the team stepped forward.

"All of you, all of US, have voted for new governments many times. Have we not?"

"Yes!"

"Both State government and the Government in Delhi. Yes?"

"Yes!"

"Has any government that you put up there delivered what they promised? ANY government so far?"

There was a moment's pause. The crowd had not thought about this ever before. Then, in a mighty roar, the reply reverberated around the playground, NO!!! The third voice now came in.

"Has there been any difference – ANY difference – between the promises of one party and another? Roads? Water? Prices of daal, rice and wheat? Vegetables?"

"NO!" And the anger was beginning to kick in. The fourth voice came in.

"Why not? Have you ever thought about it? Why not? Why they all promise the same things, and why none of them delivers?"

This time there was a volley of responses, guffaws thrown in between.

"They got it for themselves!"

"Chor! All of them!"

"India shining!"

"All of them getting fat!"

"Bandicoots!"

The monitor flashed in red:

GIVE TIME.

The team egged the crowd on, inviting more answers, more jokes. Finally, with the monitor going blank, the fifth stepped forward.

"Maybe...Maybe...All good answers...Good! But could there be another reason? Yes?"

"What reason?"

"Each election one chor is replaced by another chor."

"Chor! All of them! We told you!"

"Yes, yes, we are the fools who put them up there!" That was an elder who had seen many elections in his lifetime. The laughter that followed brought down the heat a bit. The crowd was sufficiently agitated, but in a good mood. The monitor gave the go ahead:

GO FOR IT

The sixth stepped forward now and raised his arms heavenwards. The jabber in the crowd subsided. He allowed them a few moments of silence, and then came in with the well rehearsed punch.

"There could be another reason. They do not deliver what they promise because...It is not possible to deliver!"

There was a murmur in the crowd that suggested surprise rather than disagreement, curiosity rather than rejection. Number six continued.

"The fact is...No party can deliver what they promise...Yes, they are all chor, because they are false promises. Yes, they get fat while we all struggle in the same wretched conditions. But that is because what little is possible is taken away by them. The big, big things they promise...These are simply not possible. False promises! We will soon find out more!"

At this point, the band stepped in and played the first stanza and chorus of the ever popular "Yeh hai Bambai meri jaan". The volunteers in olive green T-shirts ushered groups of participants to their respective tables.

⌘ ⌘ ⌘ ⌘ ⌘

Krishnan was up with a start. The ride in the desert was interrupted by a high pitched voice that was drowning the roar of the motorbike. "Kittu! Breakfast will be ready in five minutes. Time to get up!"

Breakfast was Amma's hot pongal and vadai, a sure hit in this home. This morning though it was not so appetizing. Krishnan was most disappointed that he was not allowed to accompany his uncle to Shastriya. Jayesh was his favourite uncle.

He took him to watch movies, he took him on treks, he gave him tuition in maths and he taught him how to strip his bicycle for servicing and put it all back. Jayesh Uncle even allowed Krish to use his prized tool box. But today...he was entertaining thoughts about revising the ranking of his uncles. What annoyed him was the secrecy. His Uncle Jayesh not telling him what the great gathering at Shastriya was all about. At breakfast he decided to ask Amma if she knew anything more. She did not. She just guessed it had something to do with the general elections in the country six months later. It was the middle of 2018 already. They had a tight schedule, preparing to launch the new party.

A new party? Uncle Jayesh? Krishnan remembered that his uncle sometimes slipped into talking about a golden future in which there would be a whole new crop of leaders, young leaders, educated, well versed with facts and figures, alive to the needs of society, that sort of thing. He always thought of this as daydreaming, and even joined his uncle in imagining other nice things in that future – no home work from school, teachers who were tops in their subjects, making a living as a singer or writer, people from other countries flocking to India to learn from us...A new party? Uncle Jayesh? He had to find out more. The first step would be to extract more out of Amma. It was clear that she knew more, but was not saying much. When he was done with the pongal-vadai he offered to clear the table. At the kitchen sink he announced that he had a free morning and would be happy to do any errands for her.

⁂

If there was ever a first-of-its-kind in Indian elections, this was it. Each table had places for up to twelve participants.

The good attendance ensured a minimum of nine per table. Most tables had all twelve places taken. On each table was a stack of blank sheets, a mug of sketch pens, a device with a keypad that looked like a larger than usual mobile phone and a computer monitor. Each table also had a facilitator joining the participants, trained to elicit maximum participation from all at the table without influencing the direction the discussion was going in any way.

The first task of the facilitator was to explain to the group what the hardware was capable of doing. You might want to know how many cars are produced every year in India, every month, every day. The facilitator entered the question into the hand held device and tapped a green button, explaining that the question may be answered in a variety of ways.

The monitor immediately showed the answers – by State, by city, by make of car, by price range and by volume of petrol consumed for every 1000 kilometers. It was then explained that in their discussion the group may want correct information for a more correct decision. They should feel free to ask for it. Would the group like a couple more trial questions? They did. One was on the price of onions over the last twenty five years. The next was about the correct procedure for registering a complaint in a police station.

The group was surprised and delighted by the bunch of answers to the question – about types of complaints, where to go, where not to go, the special provisions for women, and so on.

Subbu-sir, monitoring the prelims across all the tables, now signalled them to stand by for the start. The facilitators summarized the procedure.

Step 1. We will begin with a common question to all the tables. Step 2. The group will discuss the question to see how different people look at it, how many different kinds of experience there are. Step 3. Members of the group may ask for information, the correct information to help tackle the question. Step 4. The group can see if there is any agreed way of answering the question. The group's response will decide what the next question will be, and what direction the group's discussion will take. Any doubts? Yes, that is correct. The different tables may go in different directions after the first question, setting their own directions.

The band on the stage struck a crescendo, the brass, the electric guitars, the drum set all together.

The first question was introduced:

WHAT WOULD YOU LIKE TO DO THIS DIWALI?

There was a ready and free flow of ideas. The facilitators helped putting all the responses into a few categories – clothing, household purchases, holidays, gifts for others, food and feasting, and so on. This was followed by a bit of arithmetic. How much would it cost if a person went for all of the things wanted. They loved it. They attacked their lists with glee, helping each other with cost estimates. When in doubt they sent the question up to the Process Console. Back came the answer promptly. Each member of the table now had a Diwali list and a total cost. Some of them even joked about it being a dream. How could they afford it all? The opener had worked. The facilitator said "Exactly", and then posed the next question:

WHERE WILL THE MONEY COME FROM
FOR ALL THIS?

The training camp had prepared the facilitators for a backlash at this point. How could anybody throw cold water on a warm Diwali dream? The group might feel offended and walk out. They did not. There was a hint of an awkward pause and then they joked about it: What prevents us from buying on credit? Or borrowing money?

It is Diwali after all! The first hurdle crossed, the facilitators were now confident of sailing through the flow chart for the day.

⌘ ⌘ ⌘ ⌘ ⌘

Krishnan had a brainwave. Dabbu's apartment block overlooked the Shastriya grounds. They would sometimes watch a Zonal League cricket match from the balcony of the flat. For an even better view they would go to the terrace of the building. He had to get Dabbu to join him. He cleared the kitchen sink in ten minutes, got the required nod of approval from Amma, and dashed off to Dabbu's on his freshly cleaned and oiled bicycle.

⌘ ⌘ ⌘ ⌘ ⌘

The tables were now approaching the culmination of the morning exercise. Exactly as announced at the start, the discussion around the first question had led to more questions, chosen entirely by the table. Without anybody telling them in so many words, without a single word used from the vocabulary of those people in high offices, all the participants at all the tables were now completely clued into what was possible and what was not as a National Diwali Budget. The thought that crossed the mind of every participant was where all this was heading? What is this new party getting at? Many found the emerging picture disturbing. "Why are we continuing with this?" was a common refrain in most tables. But they continued anyway. It was disturbing, but it was exciting finding out how the world worked.

Jayesh had placed himself at the bandstand stage. He was in constant touch with Subbu-sir at the Process Console. It was going well. They exchanged smileys often. The penultimate round was now on. The tables were zeroing in on an agreed list of demands to be made to all political parties, whether or not they were in power. The demands were for answers to six basic questions they had arrived at, based on what they had learned in the past hour. The six questions might differ from table to table in wording, but a common undercurrent was now detectable.

Jayesh noticed a steel grey SUV drawing up near the gate. It entered the Shastriya ground, did a tight circle and headed out again, pausing briefly at the gate before speeding away. It was difficult to see who was in the SUV. Subbu-sir noticed it too. As a matter of routine he flashed a message to SAT.

⌘ ⌘ ⌘ ⌘ ⌘

Krishnan and Dabbu stood their bicycles against the pillars in the basement parking area and raced to the lift. There was a hand printed sign that said it was closed for maintenance till 1pm. They tried the service elevator, but it seemed to be stuck mid-way at some floor. They took the stairway and rushed up to Dabbu's flat to pick up his father's binoculars. Another dash and they were on the terrace at last.

⌘ ⌘ ⌘ ⌘ ⌘

Subbu-sir now gave the go ahead to all the tables for the last stage of the exercise. It was a very satisfying moment for the person who had programmed the whole exercise meticulously, foreseeing every possible direction the tables might take, assembling the data base for them, and designing the response system for the participating tables. He was seen giving two thumbs up to Jayesh on the stage. The band was asked to stand by. The last stage of the exercise would get all the tables to see that they and they alone had the right – as well as the wisdom – to tell a political party what to do if it was elected. And what to say in an election speech. In other words, to shut up and listen for a change.

Krishnan grabbed the binoculars from Dabbu and panned the Shastriya grounds. There he was! Uncle Jayesh was on the bandstand! He shouted out, "Uncle Jayesh! Uncle Jayesh!" although he knew he would not be heard. Dabbu had an idea. Why don't they light a cracker bought for Diwali? Jayesh Uncle might hear that and turn this way. Off he went to fetch a nice big tennis ball sized cracker appropriately called Atom Bomb. They first lit a sparkler, and with it they lit the long fuse of the bomb. It did not disappoint.

Jayesh heard the bang. He turned in the direction of the apartment block. Just then the bandstand turned into a fireball. The flash of white and orange reached the boys on the terrace a few seconds before the sound of the thunderous explosion. Krishnan first stood stunned, then broke out into screams. "Uncle Jayesh! Uncle Jayesh!!"

The fireball spread rapidly in all directions. It swallowed up the Process Console, the meeting tables, the reception desks. The teams playing the volleyball match first stood still and stared, and then saw a shower of flaming debris landing on the adjoining basketball court. The next moment another shower landed on them. Dabbu and Krishnan watched them run towards the gate. They were the only moving figures in the playground, a party of twelve runners in flames, collapsing one by one before they reached the gate.

[The story has drawn from the work of America Speaks, aimed at wide public participation in policy making. The national elections of 2014 brought hope to many in India, expecting a stable government at the Centre. Very soon the government enjoying a comfortable majority turned into a majoritarian form of governance. Disillusionment set in quickly.]

The Plan

He was born on a Tuesday. He was named Mangal. The full name in his school leaving certificate was Mangal Parkash Haridas Parkash Sharma. In this Sharma family the second name Parkash was added to the first name of every male member. Mangal's father, Haridas, had insisted on adherence to the rule for every one of the five sons, saying they could not be Sharmas without a Parkash. Mangal died on a Tuesday too. He was seventy six, he had lived a full life, and he had three apartments he could call his own, jointly owned by Kamini-behen, his wife of fifty years. His daughters had been settled. The son had done well in the US although they heard from him only once a year on Diwali morning, and he was completely prepared, they believed, for his departure. Tuesday was Blue day, the day of his favourite colour. He had secretly wished he would go on a Tuesday. He prepared for it from the previous Wednesday, the not so appealing Green day, and most satisfyingly the end came on the following Tuesday.

Mangal and Kamini had their first child when he was twenty seven, a little less than a year after they married. They had decided they would be done with the community obligation of producing offspring within five years, perhaps a maximum of six. The target was three. They appeared at regular intervals within the planned period – a daughter, a son, a daughter. The next two milestones in the Mangal Parkash plan were a car and a flat. The Maruti 800 came from their own savings. The flat in a new apartment complex came from a housing loan at a concessional rate from the Public Sector bank where he worked. He had reached a managerial staff position, and was eligible for the loan. He took the loan. It was all according to the plan.

Mangal and Kamini-behen personally supervised the interior fittings in the new flat. She took care of the kitchen and the puja room. He took charge of the two bedrooms, the spare room and the bathrooms. He paid special attention to the shelves and cabinets reserved for himself in the bathroom. They would hold seven soap dishes, seven toothbrushes in a stand specially crafted to hold them, seven face towels and seven bath towels. Mangal was very particular about there being one for each day of the week. The face towels and bath towels were all uniformly white, with the days of the week embroidered along the edge. When folded and kept in the cabinet, the day of the week faced the opening and was seen clearly. The soap dishes and toothbrushes were of different colours, the days of the week represented by the colours of the rainbow. Tuesday was Blue day. The house warming ceremony was on a Tuesday.

Next to the towels in the cabinet were the pajamas, all white, and the undergarments, also all white. The vests were without sleeves, called Sandow banians by Mangal. Nobody in the family knew why he called them Sandow. The chuddies were called boxers by Mangal and knickers by the rest of the family. Like the white pajamas, these were also stitched by the family tailor from poplin fabric selected personally by Mangal from the cloth market. Face towels, bath towels, vests, chuds, pajamas, they took two shelves of the cabinet.

The steel almirah in the bedroom had back up stocks for all the items. At any given time there had to be at least two of each item as back up in the almirah. Mangal had found that going to the tailor once in two years was sufficient for the required stock.

Every morning Kamini-behen made sure that the laundry basket had one piece of each of the items above. In the evening she made sure the washed items went back into the cabinet, each piece going to the bottom of its pile and finding its way to the top over the next six days.

You will ask if there was something wrong with Mangal. Many have asked the question, some even directly to Mangal. His reply has been always the same. What was wrong in having order in your life? Could there not be something wrong in your own life if there was no order in it? But why seven, they might ask. Very few know that Mangal could write a dissertation on the number seven. He had a large collection of one-liners too, used mainly to put an end to the questioning. But why seven, a guest at a wedding asked. Mangal pointed to the mantap and asked in return, "why do they take seven steps to complete their wedding vows?" Oh, Mangal could be mischievous too. A conversation with a high ranking officer in the State Government led to the predictable question. Mangal stared at the gentleman as one does while sympathizing with an imbecile. He took the gentleman aside, dropped his pitch and spoke into his ear. He asked if the gentleman knew about the seven energies? No? Then perhaps he should find out. Mangal could only give him two clues. First, Nitrogen had the atomic number 7. Second, in a pair of playing dice, the opposite sides of a cube always equal the number seven when added. Long pause. Mangal excused himself and joined other guests. Last heard, the officer in question had converted several fellow bureaucrats to the quest of the seven energies.

Mangal did not like travel. "I am a domesticated old dog" he would say. "My place is here. You people go ahead and enjoy the trip. I will stay back and look after the house. Like a faithful old dog". The in-laws in Delhi had given up. When they moved into a flat in a newly developed Trans-Yamuna colony, they had a grand house warming ceremony. All branches of the family tree were present. To avoid the snub from Mangal they sent word politely through Kamini-behen. They knew he was not going to be there anyway. Kamini-behen had come up with a suggestion that she thought might work. Why not a special pack only for out of town trips? It would have a single white tooth brush and a single white soap dish. The towel, undergarments and pajamas in the pack could be in a colour of his choice, exclusive for trips, and never get mixed up with the weekly set. It did not work. To be fair, his reply was in the softest tone accompanied with a gentle caress, his forefinger running down her spine. "Sochna padega".

⁂ ⁂ ⁂ ⁂ ⁂

It was the month of Sravan. The appointment at the Shri Bhagwati multi-speciality hospital for a complete head to toe medical check-up was confirmed simultaneously by e-mail and a message on his phone. As Mangal entered it on the calendar on the wall he saw that it was a Wednesday, and it was the day before Amavasya.

"Kamini! How can they do this?"

"Do what? Who?"

"The hospital has given me an appointment on a Wednesday."

"Aahh, your green day! Nothing to worry about."

"But it begins with Amavasya night!"

"Ohho! But the day before is Tuesday, no. That is when your body will be in peak condition. I will make sure you get the best three meals of the month that day. On Wednesday morning you will go for tests on an empty stomach, no. Only the best things of Tuesday will get examined."

She got him to see that it was possibly the reason he got the appointment so early. Most people had to wait for nearly a month. Nobody wanted the day before Amavasya. Her turn for a gentle caress, her forefinger running down his cheek to the tip of the chin.

They both used their forefingers as often as needed. Not in the presence of the children, of course. Mangal calmed down, but it was clear to Kamini-behen that he was still restless. She had learned over many years that his right ear twitching was a sure sign of restlessness, no matter how controlled he appeared to others around him. The twitching continued through dinner.

Dr. Shukla, the family physician, had suggested that Mangal should take the full check-up, and that he should take it as early as possible. He had also recommended Shri Bhagwati because of their state-of-art diagnostics. In a separate chat with Kamini-behen he had expressed his concern that Mangal was not looking too good. Not looking good? Could the good doctor explain? Dr. Shukla said he would be happy to talk about it at length, but after the full check-up.

ꕥ ꕥ ꕥ ꕥ ꕥ

The reports came in one by one over three days. When they were all put together the folder was an inch thick. It was the Premium Health Check. The standard version had all reports in by twenty four hours, and the folder was less than half an inch thick. Dr. Shukla called to say that the appointment for Mangal-ji for discussing the reports had been fixed. Dr. Shukla would be there himself as the family physician.

It was exactly as Mangal had imagined it. An inquisition. A military court martial came close to that. There were three of them on one side of a large desk with a scatter of stainless steel instruments of torture. The Chief Prosecutor was in the centre, his head bent and his eyes glued to the lines in the report, lines highlighted in yellow. The two others on either side had the practiced smiles specially reserved for recipients of bad news. Mangal sat erect, his clasped hands resting on the desk. Dr. Shukla sat by Mangal's side. They all waited quietly for the Chief to look up and speak. The Chief coughed softly four times, readjusting his reading glasses after each cough. Finally, there was a long sing-song hum and he looked over the reading glasses to catch a proper look at the person who was the subject of the filed papers.

Aahhh, this is the body we are dealing with, he seemed to be saying. His glance flitted rapidly between Mangal and the papers before he straightened up to speak.

"Good afternoon, Mangal-ji". The greeting was repeated in murmurs by all the other men in the room. Mangal felt tense and moved his neck up and down twice to ease it. He moved it left and right. Dr. Shukla took out the plastic water bottle from his bag and kept it before Mangal. He took a few sips. "No need to be tense. This will take about fifteen minutes. Relax". That made him more tense. He took a few more sips "We will get right down to the point", the Chief said. At that point he moved the folder from behind the edge of the table on his side and placed it on the table surface. His two co-prosecutors took sideward glances at the open folder.

Mangal heard the Chief's pronunciation of the verdict reverberating all around the room: Guilty! He heard heavily booted footsteps of a security squad coming to a halt outside the door. He found himself begging for an hour with Kamini-behen before being packed off to the concentration camp a hundred miles to the north. Would he be permitted one last meal? With two shots of his favourite rum? He clung on to the chair as the security squad arrived to take him away. Two of them held the chair down on the ground, as two others ripped the body of Mangal off the chair below him, like a length of Velcro. Mangal screamed hard, but was not heard. His throat had gone dry. The harder he tried, the more silent his voice sounded. He closed his eyes tight and pressed his hands over them. He told himself he would remain that way till he was blindfolded before the firing squad. The rest was darkness.

Mangal felt a hand on his back, rubbing gently. He heard a voice asking him to drink some more water. It was Dr. Shukla, assuring him that it was all right, and not so serious after all. The Chief was waiting patiently, smiling. So were the co-prosecutors.

Dr. Shukla asked the Chief to continue. "May I?" asked the Chief. Mangal straightened himself, drained the water bottle and nodded his consent.

Piles. Also known as hemorrhoids. The Chief proceeded to explain Mangal's condition to him. First, a correct understanding of what they were, what they were not and, most important, what they might be in the case of Mangal Parkash Sharma. There was a porcelain model of the rectum, sliced length-wise, to show the working parts of the expelling mechanism. He explained the classification of internal hemorrhoids into four stages of severity. Mangal's case had apparently crossed into the third stage and might well be knocking on the doors of Stage Four. No, no, no surgery yet. The Chief recommended an intensive treatment regime for four months. They would review the action plan then. He turned to the two other white coated specialists and requested them to continue. The one on the left was the gastro-enterologist. He cleared his throat, indicating that he was ready to take over. He looked towards his colleague for approval to begin. The one on the right was the neurologist. He suggested that the gastro person may do the rest, and he could come in later if needed.

The piles had to be understood in their totality, he explained. All the complaints that Mangal had reported to the family physician over the last year were interconnected. They might all well be manifestations of one larger condition. The piles were not to be seen in isolation. They were symptoms, the outward signs. The real problem might be something else. Yes, the acidity, the irritable bowel syndrome, the swinging back and forth between constipation and diarrhea-like motions, the increasing frequency of acid reflux heartburn, the dryness in the mouth and thirst, these were not to be treated as separate complaints.

The neurologist's finger went up. He added that in a secondary set of connections, even his drowsiness, the migraine headache and the ringing in the ear might be part of the same condition. It was the only time the neuro spoke in the entire meeting, but he scored. Mangal thought he spoke with great authority.

And the halitosis, added Dr. Shukla. And the halitosis, echoed the gastro. Mangal listened with awe and wondered how so many of his problems in the last year and a half were rooted in one spot down there. A small, lumpy mass at the end of the long hose packed in his abdomen.

"We come now to the bleeding..." The pause and the sideward glance at the Chief did not go unnoticed. Mangal prepared himself for what was to follow.

"Right now there are traces of blood. From what you said it is not regular either, about three times a week. There is every chance of the bleeding increasing. We must do something about that right away. There are basically three lines of action we recommend for you. They will proceed simultaneously. May I continue...?" Mangal nodded his consent.

The very first step was to get a set of absorbent plugs now available in the market, specifically designed for such bleeding. No, they were not diapers, Mangal was assured. The plug was just that, a plug. The size of half a gulab jamun. The plugs were convenient, hygienic and completely safe. The hospital lab would be happy to show him how to use them. Next, he should undergo a colonoscopy as soon as possible. It was certainly a necessity to get a fuller picture. They had to rule out the possibility of something more sinister happening in the colon, not detected by the routine examinations.

"Could it be...?" Mangal started to ask

"Maybe not" said the Gastro, quickly followed up by the Chief with "But then one never knows, and one should not take chances."

Third, there would be a course of customized medication that would tackle the whole condition over and above the individual symptoms. It would require carefully calibrated dosage and monitoring on a day to day basis. This would be explained presently.

Finally, they would put him on a strict diet and exercise regimen. The exercise Mangal could take. The diet was something to be understood better. Could he ask a few questions? Of course, the Chief interjected. Mangal posed his first question. It was really the only question.

"What about..."

"No alcohol", the Gastro cut in, anticipating the question. "Strictly no alcoholic beverages. At least through the course of medication over four months". "Not even...?"

"No exceptions, I am afraid". There was a finality to the reply that got Mangal to withhold the two other questions in his mind. The Chief softened the verdict by saying they should first ask Mangal to describe his current alcohol intake in some detail – what he drank, how often in a week, and what quantities. And he had to be utterly honest.

"Six days a week."

"Is that the average, or do you have a chosen off day?"

"I don't drink on Tuesdays."

"And on the remaining six days...?"

"Divided over rum, beer and whiskey."

"How do you decide what you will have?"

"The days are fixed. Wednesdays and Saturdays are whiskey days, Thursdays and Sundays are beer days, and Fridays and Mondays are for rum. No drinking on Tuesdays."

"And how much do you take of each of these in one sitting?"

Dr. Shukla, an occasional companion, especially on Sundays over beer, chipped in on Mangal's behalf. He was very strict with his intake, Shukla-ji assured the three other doctors. He took two drinks of the spirits or two cans of the beer. Nothing could make him pour an extra drink ever, whatever the circumstances, whoever might be present. He was disciplined to a fault.

The Chief appeared impressed, but wanted to know more. He asked what one drink meant, how much went into it. Mangal turned to Dr. Shukla and jerked his head, meaning he could speak. The good doctor continued. Years ago, when Mangal-ji created his weekly bar time table, he took a trip to College Street where you have book shops on one side of the road and a line of shops selling all kinds of laboratory apparatus on the other side. He picked up a beaker calibrated in five milli-liter steps. So, how much was poured as one drink? Another glance at Mangal, another nod. Precisely 55ml. for the first drink, and 40ml. for the second.

The trinity waited for the explanation. Dr. Shukla continued, saying that the first drink was with an invocation of Lord Ganesh, who kept an eye on the whole room from his corner pedestal. After the invocation Mangal-ji offered the first sip of about 5ml to the Goddess of the Earth, and poured it into the flower pot kept specially for that next to his armchair. Thus the total consumed was precisely 50 plus 40, which was 90ml. Not a drop more.

Encouraged by the support he was getting from Shukla-ji Mangal picked up the courage to ask the two questions he had held back.

"When do we...?"

"Straight way. The medication can start from tomorrow. In fact tonight, if you can pick up the drugs. It will be in two stages.

We will start you on a short course for a week. By then we will have your colonoscopy results fully analyzed. That will decide the more customized treatment in the second stage."

"And the colonoscopy...?"

"I suggest you take an appointment on your way out. As we said, the sooner the better. Any other questions?"

"Yes... Actually, no. Thanks. No other question."

The appointment for the colonoscopy done, Shuklaji offered to drop Mangal home and pick up the medicines for him. He did more than that. He called Kamini-behen and asked if she could join him at the café close to the pharmacy. He wanted to explain things to her personally. Shuklaji knew that the medication was going to get more complicated after a week.

Meanwhile, Mangal started work on a Medication Planner. With a little bit of searching he could locate the right ice trays for the fridge. Large trays, but for small cubes of ice. He found a dealer who had just what he was looking for, and was willing to sell just the trays. He bought two of them. The tray had compartments for 28 cubes. There were seven columns, one for each day of the week, and four rows, which Mangal marked as morning, afternoon, evening and night. All his medication would be put into the 28 compartments. He took the second ice tray, took out the compartments and fashioned a lid for the first tray. He did that by cutting a strip of rexine about an inch wide and the length of the tray. With the second tray kept face down on the first, he had a perfect box for all his week's medicines. He glued the rexine along one side of the box, with the strip stuck half and half on the upper and lower trays. The Medication Planner was ready. Mangalji was ready to take on Shri Bhagwati.

The colonoscopy was short, but not sweet. The result was not unexpected. The action was swift. The medication commenced soon after the clean up. It was complicated.

Mangal Parkash Sharma died on a Tuesday. It was as he had wanted it. There was time to inform everybody. They arrived well in time. The daughters, the sons-in-law, the grandson and the grand-daughter. There were two representatives from Delhi, from Kamini-behen's side. The son arrived too, with the Italian-American wife he had kept hidden all along. The end came hurtling at him, but Mangal-ji was not unprepared. The security guard formed the advance party. He welcomed them with a smile and asked to be excused for not rising. He requested Shuklaji to offer them a last drink on his behalf before being carried away. A tot of his favourite rum. There was no need for blindfolding, he added. He was ready for the firing squad, He had prepared for it from the previous Wednesday. It was all according to plan.

The Pulse

First there was sweating. I got out of bed to switch on the fan. It was already on. I raised the speed and went back to bed. The sweating subsided in a minute or so, but there was a lightness in the head with a dimming vision. A swimming vision would be more correct. My left hand reached for the right wrist involuntarily to check the pulse. It appeared slow. Slow and soft. While I was thinking whether or not to wake up Rupa I could also feel the pulse getting slower. And softer. Should I, should I not...it stopped altogether. I heard myself grunt. Then it went blank. Were my eyes open? I could not make out, but I could not see. I could not feel anything. I knew my left hand was still on the right wrist, but did not feel it. Neither could it move away. No limb moved. I could not turn. I sensed layers of darkness encircling me.

Rupa must have been awakened by the grunt. I heard her turn and ask if I was all right, if there was something the matter. I heard her. I could hear the rustling of the sheet, the light switch clicking on, and her voice asking once again what it was. I knew her hand was on my shoulder, shaking me gently, but I did not feel it. I only heard her voice. I so wanted to reply and tell her that it was over, but the words stayed within. She rushed out of the bed. She called a number and then a second number. She was in panic. She called a third. I heard all of it. I saw nothing. I heard everything. And then she left the room. At that moment I felt a sudden need to hear her voice. I did not want it to stop. I had to know I could still hear. I had to know how long it would last. I had to know if I was really hearing her voice, or was it...what could it be? Did it matter what it was? I could still hear things. I could not see things, feel things, but I could hear.

So this is it. I have seen what it is like. You lose everything you were ever conscious of, ever sure of, everything you thought belonged to you. You are left with just one thing. You do not have a choice. It is a gift, it is given. I was given hearing. Why, I will not know, nor ever question. All of what I thought was mine was gone. Except hearing. Is someone else left with something sense? Smell? Touch? I wonder how that might feel. I don't think I will ever know. I may soon lose the thought of the question itself. Only hearing may remain. I do not even know where the hearing resides. Sometimes I listen. I hear voices then, from a far off time, from away places. At other times, when I am not listening, I hear music. Glorious music. It can keep me going forever.

⁂

The music was unfamiliar, of unknown origin. It was an orchestral sound, no voices. I could not place the instruments, but it was as if I knew every one of them. It was glorious. I was being bathed in melody, swaddled in layers of warm notes, and carried up like a babe to be walked to sleep. The music fell behind me, following in disciplined steps, as I was drawn upwards into a tunnel opening before me. I was going up a rabbit hole I said to myself, not without some amusement, knowing that it was all to myself. As I entered the tunnel I sensed that the warm layers wrapping me were falling off, and whatever was carrying me there was dropping off. I was there, suspended, horizontal, perhaps, with no way to know the position I was in really. The music remained.

I sensed a tunnel of light, and I wondered at the new experience of hearing light. It was a gentle reverberation, atonal without jarring, soothing. I wondered if I was to fall asleep. Was sleep possible? I sensed an acceleration and heard the light changing colour. It was soon the sound of white, pure white, brilliant white. The tunnel was forming a trajectory now, starting upwards, but moving quickly to a curved path, moving away, away, away from wherever it began. I felt myself reducing in size as I accelerated, smaller and smaller till I was like a tiny particle in a Large Hadron Collider. The particles bombarding me were sounds, little shiny sounds. They were voices. The sound of accelerating white was overlaid with the sound of voices. I recognized them as voices, but could not place them or make out what they were saying. Little shiny sounds of voices, many voices in clusters, changing, lap dissolving from cluster to cluster.

At last, when the collider had run out of bombarding particles of sound, the passage changed. From continuous acceleration it changed to a steady state. The course changed too. It was not moving upwards and away anymore. It was in a fixed orbit. What was it orbiting around? Was it mother earth? Was it empty space? How was I to know? It did not seem to matter. I was still there, my hearing still with me, and the sound of accelerating sound now dropped to a steady sound of dazzling white. Gradually, ever so gradually, a slow deceleration set in. The sound of whiteness changed with it, bringing in tiny bits of corruption to the white. In a while, not unexpectedly, it was not white anymore. Old, familiar sounds of other hues crept in, and the light of the tunnel was replaced with the everyday sounds of the world I had left behind. The end of the tunnel was now seen, inviting an exit. It opened into the bedroom.

⌘ ⌘ ⌘ ⌘ ⌘

It was empty. There were voices downstairs. All of the upstairs had an empty sound. No sooner had I wondered about the people gathered downstairs I found myself transported there. There were some familiar voices, the near and dear ones, there were others with degrees of unfamiliarity. I could make out that they were in a circle, some seated on chairs, some on the floor. A discussion was on. I had a strong urge to join, but preferred to remain a hovering observer. One of them had taken charge, and was gently getting others to participate. It was none other than the admirable Shiv, my son-in-law. He was firm at times, but gentle in the way he laid down his firmness. He was getting the group gathered to see that it was the unquestioned desire of the departed to have the physical remains donated to medical science. Also, that it had to be done immediately. There were murmurs, but they did not disagree. Perhaps a remembrance evening. Yes and no, said the family, speaking one by one. Yes, a remembrance. But no religious ritual. Whatsoever. A celebration perhaps. With his favourite music in the background. Vinyl long playing records, of course.

A voice from the next room announced that coffee was being served. Vadai, upuma and coffee. It was done. They rose in twos and threes, showing some reluctance to close, but moving on nevertheless. It was done.

⁂

Done and dusted. It was time to move on. I had heard all that needed to be heard. I had heard enough. The tunnel had brought me to the gathering in time. I now longed for the sounds of traffic and the barking dogs, the treetop warblers. And the hawkers at the end of the road. I hovered outside the gate. The orchestral sound began. I could not place the melody, but it was glorious. The tunnel opened up before me. I was carried up once again, the music falling behind me, following in disciplined steps, as I was drawn upwards towards the tunnel. The voices faded out. The music faded out.

The Shroud

I am an atheist for nine months in a year. And then the mango season comes along. For the three months from mid April to mid July I have to lock up the rational scientist in the Godrej almirah, and release the quarantined animus from the puja room to roam free, and behold the divine manifestation in thirty avatars occupying a broad bandwidth of hues from harlequin green to carmine red. They say that the unseen divine creator, like the unseen Indian, lives in the villages, and there reside about two hundred and fifty avatars waiting to be recognized and brought home for installation. In a village in Uttar Pradesh an ardent devotee has produced three hundred varieties of mango on a single tree by specially developed grafting techniques. That is true unity in diversity. Anything can happen in Uttar Pradesh, they say. I was born and bred in the city of Bangalore. My only forays to the rural countryside have been the annual pilgrimage to Chikkaballapur where the best Badami and Mallika mangoes are grown.

My drinking buddy on Saturdays is Prof. Gurudath Haridas. Prof. Haridas is a new age management guru with a deep appreciation of ancient Indian history. He holds forth that the mango is a botanical manifestation of Lord Krishna. It was yet another clever device of the Mischievous One to enter the homes of all in the land, to be given a place of honour in the kitchen, and from there to enter their souls as they took His name in ecstasy. In the mango season, all Indians of all castes, creeds, colours, Hindu or otherwise, experience Vishnu within them. I am an unapologetic champion of the gospel of Dr. Haridas. The mango as a motif is as prominent in Tanjore temple architecture as it is in the frescos on ceilings of monasteries in the Himalayas. As the good professor is quick to point out there is much to learn about ancient management practices through the mythological tales of the mango.

We know that mankind is susceptible to a variety of air-borne, water-borne and contact-borne infections in the summer. Coping with the heat and dealing with the summer maladies at the same time can be quite trying. It is the period when mankind is low on faith and high on instant relief. Along comes the mango to restore the faith. There is even a bowl of the choicest fruit kept in the puja room. As the summer moves from the southern part of the sub-continent to the north, so does the appearance of mangos, with a distinct avatar in each belt.

⁂ ⁂ ⁂ ⁂ ⁂

The voice from underneath the blanket produced a flow of syllables in a monotone. It was punctuated by a heavy breath. It was not a steady flow, it came in bursts, the words, the breathing, the words again. They might have been measured bursts, rather like the grunt of a bullock cart wheel along a country road. It was an endless ride and had a sleep-inducing rhythm. It stopped now and then as the entire heap under the blanket took a fresh shape, and then recommenced, picking up the flow once again. It went on through the night. The ward attendant could never tell if the body under the blanket was awake or asleep. It refused attention when touched. It wished to be left alone. It was in pain. It was a pain the ward staff had never seen. It was not known what it was, a man or a woman, young or old.

An old couple, in rags and obviously homeless, had brought the body to the emergency cell at about 2 am, when the duty doctor had signed off. The lone attendant had been persuaded to take the body in at least till the first medical staff arrived, which would be some time after half past six in the morning. At first the attendant had dutifully refused. He did not know if he was allowed to and could not remember a precedent. He asked the perfunctory questions, less than half awake. The patient's name? Not known. Age and sex? Not known. From where had he been brought? There was an answer to that one. It was on the street, a hundred meters from the hospital, next to an open drain. What made the couple bring the body there? There was a pack of four dogs roaming the street. They stopped by the body and were in conference on the best way to tear it apart. The old couple tried to shoo the dogs away. They crouched and bared their fangs, and took a step forward to send out a warning. The old man took off the old blanket he was covered in and waved it frantically at the pack. The old woman added that it looked like a ghostly dance. The pack retreated, but remained on the other side of the road. The old man covered the body with the shroud, and the two of them brought the body to the hospital ward, because there was a light on outside. The attendant was in two minds. Just when he thought that he must not do anything outside the rule book he saw four pairs of eyes moving up to the steps to the ward. He heard low snarls emanating from behind the eyes. He relented and agreed to take in the body. On one condition. The couple had to take it away at six in the morning.

The attendant woke up a little after six to find that the body was still there. He looked around for the old couple. They were not there. What would he do with the body? His mind was racing. And then suddenly the thought appeared. What body, he asked himself. He knew of no body. He waited outside the steps. When he saw the morning shift replacement turn the corner and approach he waved to him and walked briskly away. He had just alighted at the bus stop near his home when the cell phone in his kurta pocket rang. It was the duty doctor. The attendant was ordered to return to the ward. He knew it was not right, he said to himself. How could he have been so foolish to let the body in? Who knows, it might be a corpse by now.

It could become a police case. God knows what complications that would bring in.

I reached the ward at about the same time the attendant did. He greeted me at the steps and dashed off inside. I wondered why he was looking so nervous. The buzz went around, "Dr. Prasad is here..." That is my name, Lakshminarayana Prasad. I am the senior consultant neuropsychiatrist at the Institute, visiting three times a week. I had hardly reached my room when the duty doctor came rushing down the corridor to tell me about a strange thing that had happened in the Emergency cell. I greeted him, adding that it was a fine morning and that I had a treat in the basket for the staff. He said he had something important to report. I greeted him again, this time adding a smile, to serve as a reminder that it is the done thing when meeting colleagues at the Institute. I opened the covering on the basket I was carrying to show him that it was indeed a lovely morning. I had four kilos of the choicest Badami, and we would all have it at lunch time. The duty doctor forced himself to nod his head in appreciation, but kept pointing down the corridor. I realized that it was something more than an epileptic seizure or delirium tremens that was causing his agitated state. I excused myself for half a minute, went into my room, placed the basket of mangoes on the medicine chest, put on my duty coat and joined the doctor outside. He led me down the corridor in hurried strides. The staff and early visitors were lined up on both sides.

There was a group of paramedical staff standing in a circle around the heap. They were quiet, but mumbling expert opinions. The scene was rather like a family group at a funeral. But there were no flowers or wreaths. Just the old blanket, which was now seen to be the rough variety issued to police personnel. Khaki-green with large brown checks. At the sound of approaching footsteps the group dispersed quickly and went back to their duties. Only the morning shift attendant and the outgoing attendant remained, seated on the corridor bench. They rose and offered their namaskars as I approached.

I asked if anybody had lifted the blanket and actually seen the person under it. The blank faces meant nobody had. There was a distinct smell of urine and some indication of incontinence. I asked for a pair of gloves and removed the blanket. It was an emaciated body of a man in rags, unwashed and unattended for many days. A quick first assessment of his condition had to be done. He opened his eyes upon his forehead being pressed, but they stared ahead, unfocused. The first good sign was that the iris reflex was working. The blood pressure and pulse rate were low, but not alarming. Most important, his liver was not enlarged, and he did not appear an alcoholic. There were lacerations on his toes that looked like the work of a sewer rat. I pointed them out to the duty doctor.

What do we do, asked the duty doctor.

"The first thing to do is to clean him up and give him a change of clothes".

"Sir, he has no other clothes".

"Put him in a pair of hospital pajamas. Give him a sweater".

"Sir, he has not been admitted. There is..."

We had to get the approval – in writing – of the Superintendent of the hospital complex. The procedure, the rules, the precedence. I told the duty doc to make an entry in the register citing my name for the authorization. We would look into procedures later. He had to be deloused, just to be safe, and the rat bites had to be given priority. The blanket had to be sent to the incinerator.

"Leave it to me, sir." The duty doctor had now come out of the conditioned state of first finding reasons why something cannot be done.

"One more thing. Give him a large B plus cocktail as soon as he is cleaned up and dressed. Repeat the next 6 days."

The doc understood. It was a hefty multi-vitamin intramuscular dose, super charged with B-3 and B-12. I suggested that his case be included in the staff clinic three days later. They brought a stretcher and carried him away. It was not a good day to call a mango party with the staff. I decided to have it with the clinic session later in the week.

It was Friday. When I reached my desk I found a tumbler of hot chai with a small stainless steel disc covering it. When the orderly appeared to take away the glass he asked if the staff meeting would be held as usual. As usual, I confirmed. The seating arrangement would be the same. I asked for the mangoes to be cut and the slices kept ready for service on saucers. They could be kept in two rows on the bench under the curtained window.

⁂ ⁂ ⁂ ⁂ ⁂

We discussed at least three cases in some detail in the staff clinics. This time the very first case was Hamid LP. The duty doctor had to enter a name for the heap in the register. While cleaning him up they got to know his faith, confirmed by Habib, the ward boy. It was he who suggested the name Hamid, saying the meaning of the name was one who is praiseworthy. This patient was truly praiseworthy for having survived. They added the letters LP because the register asked for either a surname or initials. Since he was my patient they simply put in my initials.

Hamid LP was brought in on a wheelchair. He was looking fresh, clean shaven, his hair neatly parted on the right and patted down. The ward staff had chipped in and got him a shirt and pants from the second hand street shop that operated after sunset at the edge of the hospital campus. The shirt was light blue and full-sleeved, with thin purple stripes. The pants were khaki corduroy, just visible under the hospital supply sheet covering his legs. There was a thin muffler around the neck.

The first report was by the duty doctor, the second by the nursing head, the third by the neurology intern and the fourth by the clinical psychology intern. All four reported much progress in the parameters they were trained to observe. But all four noted in their reports that there had been no progress in his cognitive functions. His face remained blank, emotionless. Although he appeared to respond to light, sound and tactile stimulation, there was no response to the spoken word, and no answers to questions posed. It was clear that Hamid's case defied classification. It was a condition nobody had seen before. Everybody in the room was looking at me to suggest next steps.

Did anybody in the room know anything about Hamid's family, his home? What he did? What he did outside work? Would they be interested in looking at Hamid not as a case, but as a person? I dialed the Director of the Institute, and asked if a psychiatric social worker could be loaned for a short period for a case specific assignment. Yes, it could be treated as official, with the time logged in.

I signaled the orderly that it was time for the mango break. He dutifully brought the first serving to me. He then went about handing the saucers one by one to all in the room. All except the case on the wheelchair. They waited for me to take the first bite. I walked up to Hamid in his wheelchair and held out my saucer with two slices of Badami. No response. "Aapke liye", I said. After a pause of six seconds that seemed like half an hour he looked up at me. There was a hint of a smile. I smiled back. I picked up a slice and put it into his hand. He smiled again, this time just a faint bit more. Very slowly, the smile not leaving his face, he raised his hand and took a bite of the Badami slice. The group gathered in the room clapped.

⌘ ⌘ ⌘ ⌘ ⌘

Have you ever wondered why once a year, every year, the price of onions soars daily over two to three weeks till you cannot look far enough up to see the top of the graph? It takes a minimum of two months to tame the beast. When it comes down, it is never what it was at the start. It settles at a rate that is easily five rupees higher. But everybody is relieved and there is no complaint. Why does that happen year after year? Well, I found out why. And it was Hamid who educated me on the subject.

Hamid was discharged from the hospital three years ago. He recovered fully. The investigations of the psychiatric social worker, Anju Cherian, were invaluable in Hamid's treatment. His rehabilitation too. His family was traced to a village in Gauribidanur Taluk. It was the most prosperous family in a community that supplied gems to jewellery centres in Bangalore and Hyderabad. There was the occasional enquiry from Jaipur. How the village came to be known for the business and where the gems came from was a story in itself. Not all of it was on record. Some of it was, in police headquarters in Bangalore. Since there had never been any trouble reported in the business circles, and since the community had maintained cordial relations with other communities in the region, the police had found no need to open the files in over twenty years. Hamid's case might easily have become sensational, attracting the attention of both the politician and the policeman. Hamid himself handled things with a deftness nobody could have imagined when we knew him only as a case in the staff clinic.

Hamid was once Syed Ahmed. He was one of three brothers in the gems supply trade. Being the elder, Syed Ahmed functioned as the Mukhiya of the family business, with the two brothers heading other management responsibilities. The SUVs owned by the brothers were the only ones in the Taluk.

Syed himself drove a left hand drive Jeep, which was his first car, and maintained impeccably. He worked twice the number of hours the brothers did, often making up for their lapses in business operations. His wife and daughter, their only child, had to admonish him ever so often for neglecting his health.

The youngest brother, Imtiaz Ahmed, better known as Munna, was not really interested in the family business. He did his job simply because it was given to him by Syed. And the income was good. He dreamt of moving with the family to Bangalore city where the real action was. His cousin knew an actor who played villain roles in Kannada films. It was just a matter of time he kept telling himself. The middle brother, Anwar, found a business opportunity in wholesale trade of horticultural produce in a cluster of three Taluks. Onion was the star product in their trade, with the reputed red chilli of the region a close second.

Syed was against the family going into the new line of business. He was especially troubled by the decision to trade in onions. Didn't the brothers know that it was the most politically loaded trade? The pricing was controlled by ruthless agents who used their power to bring even government departments to their knees. As much as they were despised in public proclamations, they were also indispensable to every political party, whether in power or out of it.

⌘ ⌘ ⌘ ⌘ ⌘

It was not long before Syed started showing signs of severe fatigue, weight loss, difficulty in concentration and remembering things. The local hakim concluded it was an anaemic condition and prescribed a tonic that he himself compounded. When things got worse they took him to a hospital in Kolar. The doctor attending him pronounced the condition as dementia, and advised them to take him to Bangalore for expert attention. Munna was given the task of taking Syed to Bangalore, which he gladly accepted. The first stop was the home of a relative, where the two brothers would refresh themselves. Munna would then seek an appointment at the clinic recommended by the hospital in Kolar. With the appointment given two days later, Munna was free to take in Bangalore with friends he was in touch with. He left Syed asking him to rest well.

When Syed awoke there was nobody in the house. He stepped outside and started to walk. Where he was going and for what he did not know. He never returned.

⌘ ⌘ ⌘ ⌘ ⌘

Syed returned to Gauribidanur when he was discharged from our Institute. That was three months after he was admitted and about eight months since he left his village, as estimated by Anju Cherian. He travelled by a bus, incognito, so that his appearance caused no sensation before he reached home. There was no home. The family had disintegrated. His wife had moved the daughter to her mother's place and then found a job in Kolar. Munna decided to stay back in Bangalore and had his wife join him there. The second brother had laid claim to the old joint family bungalow, but Syed's wife had objected. The building had two locks on the gate and a board that said "PROPERTY UNDER DISPUTE. NOT FOR SALE". Syed retuned to the bus station and stood in the line for a bus to Kolar to track down his wife, Aleena, the delicate one. When his turn came at the ticket counter he found himself immobilized. In the next instant he had switched to another line and boarded a bus back to Bangalore. He had made up his mind. He would reunite his family when he had made something of his life once again.

Anju Cherian arranged a vocational counsellor for Syed. It was not for choosing a line of work from scratch. He knew what he wanted to do. All he needed was guidance on how to go about it. The paper work with the government agencies and the banks was something he did not quite understand. He was determined that this time he was going to make his business completely legitimate, with public recognition. He would source the raw materials from the Taluks around his home village. The processing plant would be on the outskirts of Bangalore. He had lined up the export channels even before the operations were switched on.

I was invited to the inauguration of the plant. I was seated on the dais next to the Secretary of Small Industries of the State. I was introduced to the guests in the front row, which included his wife Aleena and daughter Faiza. Seated next to them was Anju Cherian. Faiza was now in charge of public relations in Syed's enterprise. I had to get used to the name Syed. He was still Hamid for me, as also for all the guests from the Institute. After the words of welcome I was invited to unveil the giant plaque at the entrance to the plant. It read: BADAMI WELLNESS PRODUCTS. We adjourned to the pandal where tea and snacks were being served. At the entrance was a long table with two rows of saucers. There were slices of the choicest Badami mango kept on them. Hamid picked up the first saucer and pressed it into my hands.

[The condition known as Pellagra, caused by a severe deficiency of Vitamin B3 (niacin), resembles dementia, but is not the same. It is completely curable. It is not uncommon in communities with chronic malnutrition.]

•••

The Spot

The first time it happened he was on his way back from Meerut when he had to spend a night in Delhi before taking an early morning train to Hyderabad. His classmate from schooldays had arranged a bed for him in a musafirkhana dormitory outside Connaught Place. It was just about one star. There were shared toilets and shared bath cubicles with doors dangling by the hinges, no towels or soaps. Each cubicle had a bucket and two mugs. The shower above was an open ended plumbing line that guaranteed a gushing flow. Two fresh sheets and a fresh pillow case were all that the management of two, husband and wife, handed over across the reception desk after the honoured musafir had made the required entries in the rexine bound register and paid up the deposit of three hundred rupees.

Rafiq was shown his bed on the first floor. The steel cot had an uncovered thin cotton mattress on a cotton dhurry and an uncovered pillow. It was hard enough to break a coconut, he thought. He pushed his bag under the bed, sat down to cover the pillow and looked around. There were a total of twelve cots, set in two rows of six each. Two ceiling fans served the twelve cots. Both were on, running at medium speed, their cranking sounds differing in pitch but joined in harmony Only one other cot seemed to be unoccupied. The room had five other occupants at that time, all lying on their beds, either asleep or meditating, staring at the cracks and peeling plaster on the ceiling. Nobody noticed Rafiq taking his place. The fresh sheet spread, he decided to lie down himself. An hour's nap would be refreshing. He could take a shower later and then step out for a hot mutton biriyani at the street side eatery.

Rafiq lay down and let his limbs go. Soon the familiar railway after-sensation was overtaking him, the body feeling the rolling sway of a moving train although lying still on the bed. He remembered people complaining about jet lag. Was it something like this, he wondered. A train lag. He was not complaining. There was nobody to complain to. He enjoyed train lags. He closed his eyes to hold the enjoyment longer. It was then that he saw a dark spot floating under the eyelid of his left eye. It was small, the size of a fullstop on a printed page. It was floating gently and seeking a resting point. It was teasing. Every time Rafiq tried to look at it directly it would dart away, but return within a few moments to float and linger once again. Rafiq soon discovered that the best way to see the spot was not to look at it. He parked his eyeballs and switched them off. The spot parked itself too, inviting Rafiq to look without looking. Very very slowly Rafiq opened his eyes and saw that the spot was now resting on the hub of the ceiling fan. The blades were turning, but at the very centre of the circular sweeps was a point that had no motion. The spot rested there.

Rafiq wondered what would happen if the fan got dislodged from the hook on the ceiling. After years of shaking and groaning it might well happen, could it not? Why had it not happened so far? There was a man in a checked green and brown lungi and a torn vest lying directly below the fan.

At that moment Rafiq experienced an unusual smell. It was nothing he had smelt before. A strange amalgam of the hydrogen sulphide of sewage drains and the vapours emanating from an overflowing public latrine.

Rafiq sat up and had the unexplained desire to go out for a smoke. He stepped into his slip-ons and hurried down the stairs. Not having a pack on him he walked over to a paan shop and bought himself a single stick of Berkeley. As he drew in his first long puff he heard a crashing sound coming from the building he had just left. The paanwala left his stool and rushed into the building. A moment later he was out urging Rafiq to go in at once. There had been an accident. More people from the street were rushing in. Rafiq stood there watching, intent on finishing the cigarette he had just paid for. Four men emerged from within carrying a man in a checked green and brown lungi and a torn vest. His face was a bloody mess. The top of the skull looked prized open. They laid the body on the pavement and tried to call a cab from the taxi stand across the street. All the six cabs parked there drove off in different directions. An elderly Sikh gentleman passing by in a Maruti 800 pulled up to ask if there was some way he could help.

⁂

The clinical psychologist introduced herself as Shalini Murthy. She asked Rafiq to make himself comfortable as she busied herself with the set up for the morning's tests. She made pleasant conversation as she moved about, asking Rafiq about his Hyderabad connections, letting him know that she had done her Masters studies in the city. Rafiq felt a rare cordiality in Dr. Murthy's conversation, not generally seen in clinics and hospitals. It was not put on as a routine. She was sincere and made eye contact frequently when he addressed her. He even found her attractive. She reminded him of his cousin Jamila, who was very close to him in the family. Dr. Murthy made him feel warm. She sat on the same side of the table as Rafiq rather than on her swivel chair, the grey coloured portfolio in her hands. Rafiq Ahmed Siddiqui, she began, opening the first page.

Dr. Murthy explained that she was only one member of a team of five who had been assigned to his case. Since she was the coordinator of the team he could expect to see her more often. Over the next week or ten days he would interact with other members of the team, sometimes one of them, sometimes two or more together. The Centre was going to do its very best in his case. They had just received the report from the retinal specialist with an all clear. Floaters in the visual field were not uncommon. The spot might be a harmless blood clot in the fluid inside the eyeball. If so, Rafiq had to take precautionary measures against future ruptures in the retina. But the retinal examination had shown no damage at all. The report was all clear. There was no explanation for the spot.

The Centre for Advanced Research and Assessment in Hyderabad was the first of its kind in all of Asia, and was already attracting world-wide attention for its pioneering discoveries in paranormal and hitherto uncharted processes in the brain. Rafiq had been referred to the Centre after the Hanuman Temple episode. The shrine was gutted in a freak unexplained fire. The fire brigade had arrived too late, and four worshippers trapped inside had been charred beyond recognition. The priest had absconded. When the police party arrived for investigations they had seen Rafiq seated under the peepal tree in a dazed state. He had been picked up for interrogation. The Station Officer went through the routine of recording a statement. He began by taking down his name. Rafiq Ahmed Siddiqui. He looked up and ordered a detention straight away. His father had appealed to the good offices of the Superintendent of the Government Medical Hospital and had Rafiq released from detention. On hearing his story the Superintendent had suggested to the Centre that they consider including him in their research study.

Dr. Murthy looked up from the Portfolio. Shifting her chair ever so slightly to face Rafiq, she smiled and said "Very interesting". She was looking into his eyes now and leaning forward. Rafiq felt as if she was gazing into his brain through the peep holes in his eyes. He wanted to turn away, but found himself transfixed. He heard her saying she would like to know something more about the five episodes so far. Beginning with the one in Delhi at the dormitory.

Rafiq was now on a reclining chair in which he felt he like he was in a barber shop. Dr. Murthy laughed and said that was a good joke. She was encouraging him to talk more. He said this chair was more comfortable and it reclined much more. He was nearly horizontal now. Dr. Murthy explained that she would be injecting something into his arm that would make him more relaxed through the session. It would help a better recall of all the episodes. She kept talking to him as she gave him the intravenous injection. She then sat next to him with a recorder so that she could talk to him without taking notes.

He began with the Hanuman Temple fire. He was passing by and saw the lady with a new sari going in with an offering. He heard screams from inside when he sat under a neem tree for a smoke. In an instant there was a blaze being spat out of the entrance. Before that there had been three other incidents – episodes, Dr. Murthy called them. In all of them Rafiq had found himself with vague sensations of a premonition, but without knowing the exact outcomes. He described each of them, first in his own words, then responding to specific questions posed by Dr. Murthy.

There was the collapse of the tent cinema, the stampede killing over thirty people. There was the Tata Sumo with the drunk driver killing three hawkers on the pavement, injuring four others and smashing into the bus stop. The fourth had been the most painful for Rafiq. It was while on a pilgrimage with the family. Just as they were spreading a chadder on the dargah... Who would have ever imagined that one so young and innocent ...He could not go on. Dr. Murthy said he need force himself to continue. But could he remember what he went through at that time? In his mind. In his body, in different parts of the body.

Dr. Murthy found that while all the five episodes had tragic ends, there were other episodes, not recorded so far, in which the outcomes were not tragic, but the aura and out of body sensations experienced by Rafiq had been the same – a sense of weightlessness, an emptiness in the stomach and a need to smoke, the foul smell. And the floating spot when the eyes were closed, coming to rest on an object that was somehow going to... There was always the deja-vu when the event unfolded before him. She brought the session to a close, but encouraged Rafiq to rest on the reclining chair as long as he wished. She moved away to a desk and fed the recorded data into a desktop computer.

⌘ ⌘ ⌘ ⌘ ⌘

When Jamila learned that in the next visit Rafiq would be held back at the Centre for two days and two nights at a stretch she asked if she may bring his dinner there. She was told that it was not necessary, but she could visit him. All meals were already arranged at the Centre. So was his stay. Only one person at a time would be allowed for the visit. Was something wrong, she asked. Was it an ICU? Dr. Murthy laughed and assured her that it was nothing like that. Rafiq was quite well and would be home soon. It was just the nature of the investigations that needed continuous measurements over thirty six hours. And they were very happy with the progress. There were just two more critical assessments to be completed. These required meticulous preparation.

Rafiq was lying on a long and narrow platform, slightly curved, that reminded him of a stretcher seen in hospitals. This was much nicer looking. And very clean. It seemed to be made of some superior grade of polycarbonate. Having done a lot of roofing fixtures in his job with a building contractor he knew polycarbonates. Behind him was something like a cement mixer, except that it was gleaming white. He joked about his looming fate in a cement mixer. Dr. Murthy said "That's Rafiq, always cheerful. His name means friendly, gentle. Isn't that so, Rafiq?"

"It must be, if Dr. Murthy says so. Nobody else told me what my name means."

Dr. Murthy was addressing the team of four others gathered at the platform. He could see that they were all well dressed, but had worn white jackets above.

Directly below, facing him, was Dr. Murthy herself. On the left were Dr. Nalini Shanbhog, a neuro-physiologist, and Dr. Mohan Dev Acharya, who was referred to as a cognitive scientist and cybernetician. Rafiq asked if he ran a cyber café. "Sort of", replied Dr. Acharya with a grin, "except that we are not allowed to download and share Salman Khan movies." On the right was Dr. Subir Kumar Sengupta, who headed a team engaged in Metadiagnostics. He explained that it meant finding a common base for different kinds of manifest symptoms under different conditions. Did that make sense? Rafiq replied immediately with an analogy that came to his mind. That it didn't matter which style of biriyani you had on your plate, they would all have cinnamon in the masala mix. "Wah!" Dr. Sengupta said he simply had to share this with his students. On his left was Dr. Ashutosh Chaturvedi, a silver haired gentleman, the director of the Centre. He did not speak at all, but carried an encouraging smile on his face all the time. He was there because he was taking a personal interest in this case.

Case? Was there something wrong with him? Dr. Murthy was quick to assure Rafiq that the word "case" was used with a different meaning. The team was actually privileged to have Rafiq with them. He was a contributor to a scientific study of great importance. Beyond Dr. Murthy was a wide glass sheet which occupied almost the whole wall. Behind the glass was a room large enough to house several desks with computer monitors and several control panels that looked like modern kitchen platforms. "Ah, biriyani time!" said Rafiq. The team of five laughed and slipped out of the room. Moments later they were in the adjoining room, moving between the kitchen platforms and the computer monitors. The lights dimmed, and soon Rafiq found himself being inserted into the cement mixer, welcomed inside by a shaadi band of whirring sounds and flashing lights. He was going to enjoy this. An important scientific study.

Back at Dr. Murthy's clinic, she asked him what he thought about the last set of tests. Rafiq replied spontaneously that he felt elated. It was like nothing he had ever experienced before. He asked when he would be told what they had found in him. If he would be told at all. Dr. Murthy's answer was a smile and a slight turn of the head. Rafiq took that to mean that it might be a long time before he knew everything.

Dr. Murthy had Rafiq in the barber shop chair again. This time she was attaching a skull cap on his head. The cap was a different kind of soft plastic that adjusted itself to the shape of his head. On the outside were twelve protruding nipples. That is what they looked like, nipples, except that they seemed to be made of copper.

Dr. Murthy attached wires with little black plastic caps on the nipples that fitted snugly on them. She then pressed each nipple so that a thin rod inside made contact with the skull. It felt like a well sharpened pencil point.

After all the pencil points had made contact with the skull she attached the other ends of the twelve wires to terminals on a gadget mounted on a trolley. Across the room was another kitchen platform with an assortment of instruments. One of them was a wide printer, more than two feet wide, with an ample supply of paper on one side and a large collection tray on the other. The most interesting part of the printer was a line of twelve thin rods, bent at the end, that moved left and right very rapidly, printing zig zag squiggles on the moving sheet of paper. He saw a trial run of the print held up by Dr. Murthy. “Fine”, she said, “we may begin”.

Dr. Murthy tilted the chair back to the fully reclining position and explained to Rafiq that the test would run for at least an hour, maybe more, that he may fall asleep, and that it was perfectly all right to sleep through the test. He only had to be careful not to turn in his sleep. To keep the head straight there were paddings on either side. Dr. Murthy also explained that she may be in and out of the room, but would certainly be there at the end. She started the machine and went across the room to check the printout. She sat at her desk and started to make entries in her log book as Rafiq lay still, relaxed, looking at the bare silver white ceiling, happy with himself, at peace with the world. Dr. Shalini Murthy was an angel.

Rafiq began to day dream. When he left the Centre the next day there would be a press coverage. Relatives from all over would drop in home, there would be telephone calls, letters. There was already some talk about an interview by a TV channel. He would insist that Dr. Murthy had to be there at the interview. She would explain all the science things. He would talk about his experiences at the Centre, all the wonderful equipment, all the nice people. What would he do with the money the Centre was going to pay him? He would buy Jamila something nice, a sari or a pair of bracelets. Why not ask her what she would like? Ami would bring up the subject of marriage. It was high time, silly boy.

The day dreaming was turning into a nap now. He was drifting into a pleasant slumber. The eyelids were limp. The spot... It peeped in mischievously from one end and started floating about. The perfumed air freshener of the room was steadily being replaced by that familiar stench. He was not sure if the stench was real, actually there at the moment, or the memory of it. He opened his eyes slowly to reassure himself that it was merely a dream. At that moment he felt uneasy in his stomach. He needed a cigarette. He forced himself to remain reclined, not to turn, not to move his head. He closed his eyes to try and regain the state of slumber.

Again the spot... Teasing, making Rafiq follow it. He opened his eyes once again. The spot came to rest at last. It was on the bindi on Dr. Murthy's forehead. She had tilted her armchair back and was resting. Dr. Murthy! No!!

Rafiq was up immediately. He wrenched out the wires, threw aside the skull cap and sprang out of the reclining chair. Dr. Murthy was startled out of her nap, unprepared for what she saw. Rafiq was banging his head on the wall. When he saw Dr. Murthy rising, calling out, he rushed out of her clinic, ran down the corridor to the lobby and was out of the building before any of the security staff knew what was happening. At the edge of the campus he wanted to stop and look back. Instead he ran without stopping all the way to the railway station. He had to be as far away as possible when... it happened.

The Tune Up

Murugesh got off the bus at Kangeyam and took a shared Tempo to the village. He asked to be dropped at the firewood depot on the main road, so that he could walk the last mile home. There really was nothing like reaching home on foot. Or on a bicycle, as in his high school days. The dirt track had not changed at all in the two years since his last visit home. The mounds of gravel placed on the side every twenty yards were still there, smaller in size now, waiting for the auspicious date when a local MLA might condescend to flag off the construction of a road connecting the cluster of five villages to the main road. Murugesh was happier with the dirt track. It was so much more home. He had felt the same in his previous visit. Taking the bend after the abandoned well and seeing the entire village in the distance was the uplifting experience you never got in the city. And then you saw the neighbourhood cluster. And then your own home. And then your loved ones at the entrance when you called out from the road that you were home!

It was seven years since Murugesh first left the village. He tried to return whenever possible in the first three years, however short the visit. It was not so easy now. He was returning after two years. He was determined to make it a long stay.

His face lit up as he approached the village, but his heart was not racing as in the past. He would not hear the bell like laughter of his beloved sister. The grandmother had departed long ago. His mother had passed away a year ago, succumbing to a TB condition that was diagnosed too late. There would not even be the excited Veera barking his welcome and getting the family out of the house. His father would certainly make up for the absence of all the others. He might have put the biriyani in the pot already. He would eagerly await the tales from the city, wishing he was twenty years younger and able to join Murugesh there. How was he to tell his father that he was in no hurry to return?

⁂ ⁂ ⁂ ⁂ ⁂

If you have heard of the Kangeyam bull, you may also know that it comes from the town by that name. Kangeyam is actually a village still. Nobody knows how it came to be called a town and given a municipality. The locals still live away from the township. Only traders and petty businessmen from other districts have started living there and calling it their town. It is a town of millers. There are the old rice mills in one quarter of the town. Mills for coconut oil, ghee and groundnut oil are scattered all over, both in the town and in the surrounding agricultural areas. They say that when you are driving down the Nagappattinam-Gudalur Highway, if you start getting the aroma of fresh ghee or groundnut oil, you know you have reached Kangeyam.

Murugesh completed his high school studies from one of the nine schools in Kangeyam. His father, a small farmer who grew ground nuts and also worked in a large farm in the sowing and harvesting seasons, had made sure that Murugesh was shifted from the Government School to an English medium school when he was thirteen and in Standard 7.

The Secondary School Leaving Certificate had a rubber stamp imprint in blue ink on the front page: ENGLISH MEDIUM. His name in the certificate was Muruga Vel. His surviving grandmother from the father's side had chosen the name herself. She had a dream even before he was conceived that there would be a boy born to the household blessed by the Lord himself. She chose the hour of the night for her son to impregnate the mother to be. The Lord of war and victory, also known as the Lord of peacocks, descended into the household to bless her, and a son was born. He was named Muruga Vel. Through his boyhood he came to be called Muruga, Murugan, Murukanna, and so on, all well known variants of the Lord's name. At home it was Murugesh.

Murugesh's father did not want him to be a farmer. He saw no future in farming, all toil and no respect. He had made up his mind that the farming line would end with himself. With Murugesh settled into a city job he would sell off his meagre patch of land to the company farm for whatever they gave him and take his entire family on a pilgrimage to Palani. Unlike other members in the family tree he had only two children. Murugesh was one, well on his way to prosperity in the city, and there was Abhirami, well settled in Coimbatore with her husband of three years and a part time job in a saree shop.

It was known that many big companies were opening big shops in the city and hiring boys from small towns like Kangeyam to serve customers. All they looked for was an English medium SSLC. Some sort of work experience was a bonus. The English teacher in the school had trained all the boys for facing the interviews by people from the city. He got the boys to grasp the importance of keeping their heads up, not looking down at the interviewer's shoes, and answering questions boldly. The key answers to most questions were memorized:

"I am knowing".
"I am learning already".
"I am doing like that only".
"I am hundred percent".

Murugesh's first job was in Gudalur. It was more like an apprenticeship. From there he crossed the border into Karnataka, as most boys from Kangeyam did, and did a stint in a warehouse in Nanjangud. From there he reached Mysore city for the first real retail outlet experience. He impressed the customers – and his supervisor – with his ability to guess what they were looking for and finding it for them. He was a favourite among them. Month after month his picture appeared at the entrance of the store as the STAFFER OF THE MONTH. It was only a matter of time that he would outgrow Mysore. It was on to Bangalore! It was the happening city that all the boys dreamed of reaching some day.

As a part of the induction the batch of thirty trainees was taken on a tour of supermarkets and malls to see how they worked. Murugesh had not seen anything like that before – the size of the stores, the number of floors, the choice on the shelves, the cartloads of purchase by each customer, the lines at the billing counters, the colours, the sounds, the smells.... Talking of which, all the staff smelt the same. The management had supplied them all with the same deodorant, both boys and girls. They were never ever to appear at the store without a generous spray of every corner of their anatomy.

The staff assembled every morning in the basement fifteen minutes before opening time, standing at ease, the toes of their shoes against the white painted line. They snapped to attention on the appearance of the Floor Manager. The checklist for the morning inspection included clean fingernails, non-greasy hair, non-sweaty face, non-dusty shoes, non-wrinkled shirt and pants and, of course, strictly no body odour. It was not unusual for a boy to give himself a second spray in the lunch break.

⌘ ⌘ ⌘ ⌘ ⌘

It is known that Tamil-speaking people had made Bangalore their home from the time Lord Cornwallis decided to establish a Cantonment there. They took care of the everyday needs of the British, providing essential goods and services that were not forthcoming from the inhabitants in the old city located within the fort area. The city people were not only content with their existence but also displayed a certain loyalty to their ruler, Tipu Sultan. The British wooed the Tamils. The Tamils reciprocated with loyalty and dependability. They came from all faiths, but they were Tamil first, and Hindu, Muslim or Christian only incidentally. Naturally, the British bestowed favours and privileges on the Tamils readily. It only widened the divide between the old city and the Cantonment.

Young migrants like Murugesh coming into Bangalore had no anxiety about settling in. There was even a Kangeyam Hostel off Tannery Road which had advance information about Murugesh's arrival. They welcomed him with a hot meal of egg curry and ghee rice.

It was in the hostel that Murugesh met Daniel. They called him Danny-anna. In his mid-thirties he was the oldest in the group. Danny-anna was not from Kangeyam and did not stay in the hostel, but was a frequent visitor there. He had two friends from the Kangeyam area who stayed in the hostel. Danny-anna was popular in the hostel and always welcome. He sang Tamil film hits, he played the mouth organ, he mimicked film dialogues, and he cooked an out of this world fish curry whenever he came. He was also giving the boys useful tips to get them street smart in Bangalore. Danny-anna got Murugesh to upgrade his moped driving license from Kangeyam to a regular motorcycle license, so that he would qualify for outdoor assignments at the retail company. He then took him under his wing and taught him to drive a car. He also arranged for female company to service him once a week.

Daniel was a driver in a wealthy home. The community was from the North, perhaps the Western part of the country, but it was the third generation in Bangalore. All members of the family managed some Kannada and some Tamil. The head of the family had some sort of export business that people like Murugesh never quite understood. The nature of the business was never seen in action, as you would in a textile mill or a hotel or a jewellery showroom.

All you saw of the boss's business was a very modern single storeyed office in a posh business district of the city. It must have been a successful business. How else could they stay in a palatial three-storeyed mansion with two separate gates marked In and Out? There was a landscaped lawn and garden that boasted prize winning roses. There were two gardeners and a platoon of house staff on call twenty-four-seven, working in two shifts. It was a joint family of two sons, one daughter and their families all staying with the boss in the mansion. There was a lift that went right up to the covered terrace where the most important dinner parties were held. There was also a separate service lift at the rear. The large common kitchen had an extension into an outhouse at the back and could easily serve a guest list of over seventy.

The boss moved about in a Merc kept exclusively for him and Ammaji. There were four other cars in the covered parking area on one side of the Out gate used by the rest of the family. One day on the morning drive to the office the boss asked Daniel if he could find another good driver like himself.

"Give me some time, sir. We can't get any driver from the street for this house."

"Correct. Take your time. But find a good man."

Daniel was sure Murugesh was the right man for the job. He took Murugesh out for dinner to Swamy's and ordered a half bottle of Triple X to be brought in from the supplier down the road. He brought up the topic while pouring the second drink. At first Murugesh thought Danny-anna was pulling his leg. Driver? Muruga Vel, Driver! Daniel was prepared for this. He first laughed with Murugesh. He then asked if Murugesh was embarrassed that his Danny-anna was a driver.

"Oh, no, nothing like that! It's just that..."

Daniel smiled and patted him affectionately. He said he shared Murugesh's anxiety.

"You are thinking what you will tell people back in Kangeyam? Is that it?"

"What is there to say? Say to whom? I have to live my own life."

Daniel knew it was working. This was the time to tell Murugesh what he got as a driver. Of course the pay was good. There were the perks. All day time meals in the mansion and a generous allowance if outside on duty. Quarters at the back if confirmed. Getting to see the celebrity company the family kept. The quantities of foreign liquor left over after parties. Four sets of uniform and two sets of polyester-wool uniform for special occasions.

"But I am raw. I don't have experience."

"Neither did I when I started."

"I don't know anything about looking after cars. What if the car stops somewhere? Or has starting trouble?

"That was all in the old days. We don't have Ambassadors and Fiats anymore."

Daniel explained that it was all about giving people confidence that he knew his job. Did he not remember the coaching from his teacher in high school? "I am knowing!" They will expect the driver to be peering into an opened hood once in a while. If asked he should simply say he was tuning up the engine. They like that. They will watch from a distance and tell their friends about the regular tune ups their cars get.

In actual fact today's cars need zero maintenance. All he had to do was to keep the spark plug housings clean and shiny from the outside for people to see that a good tune up job had been done.

Murugesh was met at the entrance by his nephew, Chinna. He told Murugesh that his father had to be present at the Panchayat meeting to which he had been summoned. Murugesh had to make himself some tea and rest. They would have an early dinner together. Murugesh decided to drop his bags there, along with the gifts he had brought for his father, and go to the Panchayat meeting himself. Chinna offered to take him to the school courtyard where the meeting was being held. When he got there Murugesh saw that the heated discussion was about his father selling his farm to the landlord in the next village without prior information to the Panchayat. It turned out that the Panchayat expected to be informed of all farm sales, its consent sought, although there was no legal requirement for such a consultation. Murugesh realized that his father was unprepared for the call and that he was at a loss for words. When the Panchayat members greeted Murugesh on his arrival he took advantage of the brief interlude to seek their permission to say something. Of course, they said, he was welcome to join the meeting, they said, asking if he would like some chai and bakery biscuits. Murugesh was in many ways a model son of the village. It was good to see him back, city clothes and all.

Murugesh simply requested the Panchayat to give his father more time. Putting his newly acquired diplomacy to good use he said he had returned to meet his father for precisely that – to help him to decide about the land. He apologized on behalf of his father for any misunderstanding, asserting that it was entirely inadvertent. The Panchayat was pleased. One of them said they knew all along that it must have been an innocent mistake. Another said the village needed more sensible young men like Murugesh, and that he could easily be part of the Panchayat if he was staying on. Murugesh smiled. He said he was honoured by the remark, even if merely a sentiment. The meeting closed on a cordial note.

⌘ ⌘ ⌘ ⌘ ⌘

Danny-anna succeeded in getting Murugesh to make the change. His coaching in driving habits was really valuable. Very soon all in the mansion were talking about Murugesh as a Daniel Junior. Driving for a living was a different experience. It was turning out a good experience. Once in a while he got to drive the Merc.

The trouble started with the son-in-law's change of tone in talking to Murugesh. It was not there at the start. He was the one who spoke the least to Murugesh, but at least there were no negative signals then. He was called Dhirajbhai by everybody, Dhiraj-sir by Murugesh and Daniel. Dhirajbhai's wife, the daughter of the boss, was different. She was friendly and kind with Murugesh, even sweet. Lily-behn they called her. When he drove her out she sometimes sat in the front, asking others to take the rear seats. On some occasions she even asked Murugesh to sit at the same table when she took a snack break.

Maybe that was the problem. Dhiraj-sir had opinions on many things, but Lily-behn had a mind of her own. Lily-behn was warm and friendly with everybody, was she not? Even Daniel. Murugesh often thought about that. He once told Danny-anna that Lily-behn laughed too readily. What did he mean? As if she was filling up some emptiness, he said. Danny-anna did not want to get into that, but said that a laughing behnji was always more welcome than a scowling behnji. Murugesh knew what he meant. You could not say much about the rest of the family. It was a strictly a master-servant relationship. He was a driver. The family was not rude or unreasonable, but they were not friendly.

The rest of the household staff were distant, much older, and regarded Murugesh as an import item. He was beginning to get lonely in the mansion.

It was different at the mall. There were lots of boys and girls on the floor, and they were all his own people. Murugesh wondered if he should confide in Danny-anna. He decided later not to, anticipating his familiar advice that it was all a matter of adjustment. He also sensed that the boys in Kangeyam Hostel were not as chummy as before. One Sunday, when he had the evening off and the boys had chosen to go to a movie without him, he sat by himself in the hostel and reached for the half full bottle of Scotch from the mansion. He thought he needed a drink. But he was angry with himself that it had to be the whiskey from the mansion. After his second drink he broke into a song from his school days. It was the song of the cowherd who has just sold his Kangeyam bull to a farmer, asking him to take good care of his beloved bull. He was in tears as he ended the song. And poured himself a third. Just then there was a knock on the door. He sat up and went to the door. It was Danny-anna. He had sensed that Murugesh was not his usual cheerful sense and had decided to keep him company through the evening. He came to the point. What was it?

Murugesh did not have the words to describe the despair he was going through and the furious exchange that was on between his head and heart. Daniel listened to his restless rambling until it was spent. Murgesh was bent and sobbing into his palms again. Daniel waited for him to stop, his arm around his shoulder. He then took out a packet that he said was sent by Lily-behn for him. Murugesh straightened himself. It was a bar of imported chocolate. Her brother and sister-in-law had just returned from a trip to Europe with a large hamper each for the two other branches of the household. Lily-behn decided she did not need so much chocolate for herself. Mrugesh was in tears again, this time calling out to his namesake god to take him away. Daniel waited for the storm to pass and got Murugesh to talk about it.

At first it seemed like the loneliness Daniel had gone through himself in his first year as a driver. Murugesh was missing the company of his own people in the mansion. Soon he detected another current flowing underneath. It had something to do with the lavishness and wastefulness in the mansion. Murugesh first felt sad that the lives of the people there were so completely cut off from the real world of real people all around them. But he realized that they had very nicely created a world of their own, with their own kind of people around themselves, finding their own ways to keep up their unreal lives. Daniel asked him to explain. He did, by asking Danny-anna in return if he had ever seen what went into the three gigantic garbage bins every morning. Had Danny-anna forgotten how the boss and Ammaji take a walk? When they take the service road for an evening tea at the neighbour's? Danny-anna had to follow them in the Merc, driving at their walking speed. Did he not know that every bedroom had air-conditioning throughout the year, and that every bed had blankets and quilts throughout the year? That a month's electricity bill in the mansion was…

"More than my salary for three fourths of a year", Danny-anna completed the sentence for him, letting him see that he understood, encouraging him to continue, the hand back on Murugesh's shoulder. What made Murugesh sadder was the fattening of the household staff, aligned to the same mindlessness.

One day, returning from a trip to the supermarket, Murugesh was asked to leave a packet of toiletries in the bathroom attached to bhabiji's bedroom on the first floor. He entered cautiously and saw that the bathroom door was open. He was stunned breathless. It was nothing he had ever seen, not even in the scenes of rich homes in Tamil films. First, the vastness, the bathroom space greater than the whole dorm in Kangeyam hostel. There was a separate dressing room on one side with wardrobes along an entire wall. That is where he stood, next to an upholstered bench of carved teak. He had to take a step down into the area where people bathed. It had two separate arrangements. First there was a glass and gold bird cage with a shower inside. Next to it was what looked like an oval swimming pool of marble sunk into the floor. There was a large cane basket with fresh rose petals. Murugesh imagined the water in the pool covered with the rose petals. There were flower vases everywhere with freshly plucked blooms from the garden. Flower vases in a bathroom! Another upholstered bench between the two bathing spots had three stacks of towels of different sizes, in different colours. And above.... the whole ceiling was a mirror. Turning left he saw the area where people relieved themselves. It had two wash basins on one side and two seats side by side. He wondered if two persons sat there side by side. He thought the second seat looked different, but was not sure exactly how. All the ceramic fittings were gleaming black. All the plumbing fittings were gold. The flooring was blood red, with gold piping between the tiles.

He kept the packet on the bench and dared to walk around the toilet seats and wash basins, touching them lightly to see if they were real. He sat on the upholstered bench to catch his breath.

When he returned downstairs he went directly to the parking area. Opening the hood of the Toyota he buried his head deep inside in a tune up.

From that day on Murugesh looked different, he sounded different. He smiled less. People noticed that he seemed preoccupied, looking elsewhere when they were talking to him. Lily-behn spoke to Daniel about it. Murugesh had stopped entering the house through the front verandah. He would take things from the car to the house from the service entrance at the rear.

One afternoon Lily-behn instructed Murugesh to follow her with a few bags from the car as she herself carried some of them in. Dhiraj-sir was seated with his friends on the verandah. They were enjoying a leisurely spell of beer and wine before lunch. The mansion was nearly empty, with the rest of the family away holidaying in various parts of the globe. Even the house staff had been let off. As Murugesh stepped into the house he overheard the conversation on the veranda.

"Smart driver."

"Yeah, Lily likes the bugger."

"That is important, na? A driver should be like part of the house."

"As long as they know their limits."

"What's his name?"

"Murga!" There was a guffaw. "We have a murga strutting about in this house!"

Lily-behn joined the group moments later. They complimented her on having a smart driver like Murga. Dhirajbhai laughed. She corrected them, looking Dhirajbhai in the eye, that the name was sacred, and that it had three syllables, Mu-ru-gan or Mu-ru-gesh, and not two syllables as in Mur-ga. There was an awkward pause in which Dhirajbhai glared at Lily-behn. She reciprocated with a smile of utmost serenity. One of the group asked helpfully if they should move in for lunch, and they did. Murugesh, listening from behind the curtain, sped away to the kitchen, and from there to the Out Gate. It was a daring thing to do. Daniel had the afternoon off. For two whole hours there was no driver in the mansion.

When Murugesh returned Dhiraj-sir was waiting for him at the parking area. He asked why he was not on call when a guest had to be dropped. Without waiting for a reply he went on to accuse Murugesh of negligence and arrogance and rude behaviour. The shouting turned into an avalanche of abuses.

Murugesh smelt the beer in his breath, but could see that it was coming from somewhere deeper. He mustered all his training at the mall and kept his cool, not retorting on impulse or arguing back. When there was a momentary drop in the attack Murugesh said he would reply to all of Dhiraj-sir's allegations later, in the presence of Danny-anna. As he turned to leave, Dhiraj-sir caught him by the collar, spun him around and landed a powerful right hook on his middle. Murugesh buckled in pain. Two blows in quick succession landed on his face dropping him to the ground. Murugesh looked up helplessly. Dhiraj-sir kicked him, spat at him, and moved to pick up the night watchman's five foot long lathi kept against the wall. Terrified, Murugesh cried out loud, "NOOO!! NO, PLEASE!!"

The shouting and the cries brought Lily-behn running out . She rushed to Dhirajbhai to stop him. He hurled her aside, shouting at her now.

"You keep out of this, you bitch!"

Lily-behn, down on the ground, held on to the lathi. Dhirajbhai threatened to beat her too if she did not let go. With the attention turned away from him Murugesh scrambled to his feet and lunged at Dhiraj-sir, taking charge now, one arm around his neck, the other on the bamboo staff, trying to wrench it from his grip.

"Leave her alone, sir! Leave her alone!"

Dhiraj-sir did leave her alone. He stepped back, stared at Murugesh, then at Lily-behn on the ground, then at Murugesh again. With an earsplitting scream he pounced on Murugesh throwing him on the ground. He had both his hands around Murugesh's neck. It was a fight to the finish, and Dhirajbhai had the upper hand. Lily-behn rose quickly, the lathi now in her hands. She landed the blow squarely on the back of Dhirajbhai's head. A second blow landed on his back. He rolled over, senseless. When Murugesh recovered he was in panic. This was the end of the road. Lily-behn examined Dhirajbhai quickly and assured him that he was all right. She advised him to leave immediately and begged him not to do anything foolish like informing the police. She would take care of things. She would tell the rest of the family that it happened when she had given Murugesh the afternoon off. She assured him that Dhirajbhai would never raise a complaint against him. She knew how to take care of that. It was time to go. Not a moment to lose.

Murugesh rushed to the hostel, put as many of his belongings as possible into two duffle bags and one ruck sack, changed into non-descript desi clothes, wore a bandana over his head and slipped on a pair of large dark glasses. He left a hurriedly scribbled note for Danny-anna saying only that he had to leave urgently and could not say when he would be back.

There were no buses towards Coimbatore till late in the evening, but Murugesh decided to take a chance anyway at the Inter-State terminus. He would wait till something came along. In contrast to the stillness on the bus platforms, the traffic across the road was crawling in both directions to a continuous background din of competitive honking. A sedan with tinted glasses drew up on one side of the entrance to the terminus. The glass lowered a few inches to reveal Lily-behn. She had spotted him. Danny-anna emerged from the other side and walked up to him.

He was carrying a rexine bag with a zipper. Murugesh smiled nervously, not sure about how much he knew. The meeting was short and strictly business. Danny-anna pressed the bag into Murugesh's hands with just two words, "From Madam". He turned and walked away. He thought he saw a hint of a smile on Lily-behn, followed by a short wave of a hand. The tinted glass rolled up immediately. They drove away.

Finding a fellow traveller to look after his bags Murugesh sneaked into the rest room to look into the bag. It was what it felt like. Bundles of currency, all in one thousand rupee notes. A small card of hand made paper said "Thank you." Murugesh made a hurried count. It was a whole five lakhs.

⌘ ⌘ ⌘ ⌘ ⌘

On the way home Murugesh was chided by his father for playing into the hands of the Panchayat. Who were they to interfere in his personal affairs? What could they do if he went ahead with the sale of the land? Would they be able to get a better deal for him? Noticing that Murugesh had not spoken all along the walk he asked, "Well?!"

Murugesh replied softly that he was not lying when he said he was there to talk to him about the land. Maybe he should reconsider the sale. Maybe Murugesh himself could look after the land. They walked on silently. When the house was in sight in the distance the father stopped, took Murugesh's hand and said, "I will tell you everything your grandfather taught me. No chemicals. I will show you everything."

[The explosive growth of retail business at the turn of the century led to large scale migration of young people from small towns to the cities.]

The Musical

Some enchanted evening...

Know the song? Heard it before? A great song to sing in the bathroom...

He sang in his shower. Most times it was two buckets of water and a brass pot. The shower came much later, but was only for the occasional quickie. A proper hot water bath had to be from two buckets. The brass pot had been handed down from his grandmother's time. The smell of firewood in the old bath house always reminded him of Ajji, as she had taken it upon herself to give him and his brother and sister their weekly oil bath. They were into their teens, and it was getting awkward, but Ajji had her way. There was one correct way to have an oil bath, and she gave it to them, stripped naked, one at a time of course. The Standard Operating Procedure began with application of the prescribed measure of heated coconut oil at least twenty minutes in advance. It called for a thorough wash first with hot water, steaming hot, followed by a scrubbing with Shikakai, a wash down, a clean up with neem soap, followed by the final wash. All of this was punctuated by Ajji's chanting, mostly to herself. The last potful poured on the head was accompanied by a heartfelt "Krishnarpana", and off they went. It was only when the sister dropped out that Ajji gave up the oil bath from her Sunday chores. The copper hundi embedded in a cement chula had also come from the old family home. The sister had taken away the pot on setting up her own home. It was replaced with a plastic mug. The hundi remained, but used only on ceremonial occasions when it was decreed that an oil bath needed water heated with firewood. A large capacity geyser had come into the bath house, placed high, looking down contemptuously on the hundi. A shower fitting appeared, and there were taps for hot and cold water. They appeared when the first son married and brought his bride home. The bath house became the bathroom.

The bathroom concert in those days covered a repertoire of old hits, some in Hindi, most in English, all of them classics. By default the opener was usually a faithful and perfect rendition of *Madhuban mein Radhika nache re*, exactly the way Mohammed Rafi had sung it in Kohinoor. Much loved by the family next door, but not so by Ajji. She asked why he could not sing *Lambodhara Lakumikara*, the way she had taught him when he was six. Among the hits from Broadway was the goose pimply *Some enchanted evening*. The shower permitted only one song, occasionally stretched to two. Mohammed Rafi gave way to Sinatra. On oil bath Sundays the concert had a full repertoire of at least six songs. The housewife next door sent her farmaish well before the morning coffee.

⌘ ⌘ ⌘ ⌘ ⌘

Not across a crowded room, it was across the courtyard café, created tastefully on three sides of an ancient silk cotton tree. The fourth side had a bar, open only after sunset, and an open kitchen behind that. There were flower beds snaking between tables and there were potted flowers next to every table. Miniature champa trees in large cement pots ringed the area like a sacred cordon. Not without good reason it was called Temple Trees. Not across a crowded room, it was across the courtyard café. A dozen empty tables between them, he wondered what she was doing there at noon and wondered if she might be thinking the same about him. Was that a smile on her face? He rose to walk up to her table to start a conversation, about what he did not know. Perhaps about the strangeness of their being the only two persons in the garden café. Or about the flower bed of pansies next to her table. He sat again instead.

He pretended that he had dropped something and sat down. Ah, yes, the car keys. He picked them up and rose again. He was going to leave. That was not what he wanted to do, but that was what he was doing. Leaving. He moved towards the parking lot, knowing it was against his will. But somehow he knew that he had to see her again.

It became a daily recce. To get to Temple Trees at noon, slow down before the parking lot, and look across the courtyard. No luck. Six days in a row there was no sign of the stranger. On the seventh, a Wednesday, she was there, at the same table, in the same sari with the flower prints, the same sunglasses lifted to her head. This time she had a champa above her right ear. He drove past, unbelieving, went a good two hundred meters away to avoid being noticed, turned around and returned to the parking lot. He entered the courtyard and in a fit of new found confidence strode straight to his table. He did not sit. He placed his wrist bag on the table and walked up to her table. This time he saw clearly that it was indeed a smile. She nodded to signal that he may sit.

And then it happened. He saw her face turn different. Her smile looked fiendish. She looked uninviting. The old condition of inverse libidinal response kicked in, the attraction-repulsion swing. He knew it so well, having suffered so many episodes. The condition had been with him for well over ten years. The attractiveness of a woman had an unexplained correlation with the distance. The closer a woman got to him the more unattractive she became. He loved the woman from a distance, all thoughts of desire kindled, all the warm feelings aroused. Some fantasizing was a common accompaniment. But when she was near and up close and the first conversation had taken place, he found himself turning off rapidly.

It was she who spoke first. "You looked different at the distance".

"You too", he replied, without thinking.

"I thought I should see you again."

"You were... you mean... and you came today...?"

"Took a chance. It is a whole week later, I know. I can get away only on Wednesdays at this time. You looked the type who also liked a coffee at noon?

They slipped into talking about coffee preferences, ordered two, made more conversation about coffee, the best places, the worst, and when there was no more that could be said about coffee they hit the pause button. They looked at each other properly for the first time then. They burst out laughing, realizing at once that they had both been using coffee crutches that could now be dispensed. Through the silence they knew that they needed some rules of the game to proceed further. She took the lead again.

"What next? We need some rules of the game".

Bold, he thought, but it was surprisingly not offensive. It was... attractive. But the anxiety symptoms had not left. He told himself firmly that he would count ten before making any foolish commitments. He counted to three. Like what, he asked. What did she have in mind? She offered to take the first stabs. She asked if he knew the musical *Oklahoma*. Yes, of course. And she sang the line, "Here is the gist, a practical list of don'ts...for both." But before that they exchanged short lists of musicals they loved. Five favourite musicals each, and there were three common to both lists. He was surprised she had *South Pacific* in her list. She was looking attractive again. But also a threat. She knew the songs of *South Pacific*. She tapped the table and brought the house to order. It was time to work on the house rules. She would begin, but they could both lay their cards on the table.

"We will not ask ages and birthdays. Just 'in our late fifties' should do."

"Or early sixties".

"Noted."

"We will not ask about past relationships. Just 'currently single' should do."

"We will not inflict our pathologies on each other. Just 'some problems' should do."

"But we will be frank about bad breath. If needed."

"Halitosis?"

"The rich have halitosis. Ordinary folks like us have to be satisfied with bad breath."

"We will not apologize about flatulence. Just 'clumsiness' should do."

"We will not insist on meeting daily. Wednesdays should do, blocked noon onwards."

As the list grew the items opened up more and more. They got to know each other through the house rules. They felt a lightness. They laughed. They held hands. Briefly. He withdrew gently, resisting the desire to hold on. He looked down as he wiped the beads of sweat on his brow. When he looked up again she patted his hand. She suggested that they add a line at the end of the list that it may be reviewed from time to time and revised as felt necessary by either of them. They clinked their coffee mugs to seal the deal. Two more orders of coffee, and they felt they had got to know each other well enough for a start. That would do for this Wednesday. Next Wednesday, then. Finally, before closing, they agreed on one more thing. They would have an MoU for all physical encounters to be deemed consensual.

Before calling it a Wednesday there was time to talk about what they did the rest of the week. He used to work in an advertising agency, he said. He was now a freelancer, working mostly from home. He was into photo journalism and played a Fender bass. She played golf, she said. The guys in the club were always cracking double entendre jokes around golf. Oh yes, she worked in a firm of advocates, but she was not a partner.

He thought he would die waiting a whole week. It wasn't too bad. In fact, waiting stoked anticipation, and it felt good. He slept well. He wondered if she felt the same. When he got to Temple Trees on Wednesday it was fifteen minutes earlier. There was another car parked there already. She was in it. She got out and came and sat next to him. She thought it might be good to chat for a while in the car before coffee, and plan for the afternoon. She liked the feel of his car and suggested they go on a drive.

They drove for over an hour after just one coffee. They sang. They took turns. They sang songs from their favourite musicals, all the great ones they had listed. *Oklahoma, Singin' in the Rain, The King and I, Oliver, Annie Get Your Gun.* It was something of an antakshari, except that they were singing whole songs. He was stunned by the way she belted out 'Tonight' from *West Side Story*. Then came *South Pacific*. They sang 'Some Enchanted Evening', sharing the lines between them, and joining in unison for a crescendo.

Who can explain it?
Who can tell you why?
Fools give you reasons
Wise men never try...

They stopped under a tree, near a tender coconut seller. When they got back to the car she opened her handbag and took out an envelope. It had an MoU that she wanted him to see and approve. It looked fine to him. The key section was about acceptance of mutual consent, and it was worded elegantly, part legalese, part Kalidasa. Would they need to get Stamp Paper? Did it need witnesses? Who could advise them on the procedure? It was simply an MoU, she said, not a contract. All it needed was two signatures on two copies. It could be put into operation the following Wednesday.

✾ ✾ ✾ ✾ ✾

It was time. They had got nicely comfortable with each other. They had held hands, they had hugged, they had placed a hand on the knee, then the thigh. They had kissed, ever so lightly, but ever so truthfully. They had put the awkwardness and tension behind. And there was never ever any hurry to get to things. They looked into each other's souls and knew it was time. She readily agreed to his place. He had rehearsed a hundred lines for asking, but after the kiss he simply said he wanted to take her to his place. You win, she replied.

He turned on the stereo system and played a vinyl LP. It filled the room with warmth the way only a high end system could. She picked up the jacket to see what was playing. It was "Saluting Hollywood", a collection of the great sound tracks, played by a specially arranged orchestra that had more strings than brass. The first track was A Time For Us, the Henry Mancini hit from Franco Zefirelli's film. It was played as a slow waltz. They danced. He led hesitantly at first and then more firmly. She followed beautifully. A slow zoom and the room was cut out of the field. All the crafts decorating the flat, collected from all parts of the world blurred into faint blobs. Only the faces remained, their eyes closed.

Like prisoners on death row they asked each other if there were any last minute requests. They had two requests each. They found they were the same. First, they wanted the lights off. And then they asked each other to be gentle. Neither of them was difficult to understand or carry out. After four Wednesdays trying out his and her apartments they felt ready to keep the lights on. They also agreed not to ask why they wanted the lights off earlier. They rated each other on performance. Gentleness on a scale of one to ten. The scores were satisfactorily high. It was the supreme satisfaction.

⌘ ⌘ ⌘ ⌘ ⌘

He had not sung in his shower in a long while.

"Hey there! You with the stars in your eyes..." It was a not so common tune from a lesser known musical. His voice had turned soft, but the notes were flawless. He hurried through the song because there were visitors.

The wedding reception was to be held at a country club thirty kilometers outside the city. He had put the invitation aside. He stopped attending weddings and receptions. Nobody expected him. His son from a marriage half a lifetime ago had relocated from San Francisco and taken an apartment. The son and his American wife insisted that he take an outing and they would drive him there. He agreed, not without some protestation. They made him promise he would wear a blazer, the deep blue one, and his prized Italian cravat. They called him Brigadier when he wore that.

It had been three years. Maybe more. He was content with walking in the park twice a day and watching movie classics three times a week. He could still afford Scotch and his music collection was now digital, downloaded from virus-free sites. He took out the LPs once in a while when he felt a burst of nostalgia overpowering him. That had not happened in the past six months.

The reception was at a scale he had not imagined or prepared for. He learned there were four hundred guests. They were all carrying their happiest countenances. Every corner of the vast lawn and club house patio was filled. The newlywed couple was flitting from group to group, exchanging hugs, air kisses, patting hands, moving on, leaving the group to carry on their chat from where they left it. They frowned, they grinned, they smirked, they whispered gossip, and returned to the happy faces. He felt an old panic resurfacing. It was a nervousness of unknown markings, a fear of happiness. He needed a drink.

The son and daughter-in law led him to the bar and left him there, reminding him that two large drinks and one small were his limit. They left him at the bar and went ahead with their own mingling agenda. The Scotch in his hand, he leaned against the bar to continue his anthropological observations. Nobody came to chat him up. He was not going to chat up anybody.

Across the crowded reception lawn… she was there. She noticed him at about the same time. They looked at each other for a good half minute before she smiled. He ordered a glass of sparkling white and walked up to her with the two drinks in his hands. She spoke first, as he expected, if only to say Hi. A Hi in return, and he handed over her glass. They raised their glasses, took the first sips, and then waited for some conversation to begin from somewhere. This time he decided to open.

"Why the radio silence?"

"We say that only in wartime conditions."

"It felt that way."

"Did it?"

"Three years!"

"More like four."

"I'm not early sixties anymore."

"Not late fifties myself."

Short bursts. He was making it clear that he was upset, even annoyed. She was sounding as if nothing had happened. The conversation ended. The only thing he could think of was to offer to get her a refill. He needed one. Her reply startled him.

"We should meet."

"You mean… ?" Oh god, it felt so much like their first conversation.

"It's Wednesday today" he said.

"Next Wednesday", she replied.

Temple Trees was still flourishing, but the flower beds had gone. Only two champa trees remained at the entrance, now grown large and transplanted to the ground. He got to the cafe fifteen minutes earlier. Her car was parked there already. She got out and came and sat next to him. She thought it might be good to chat for a while in the car before coffee. Yes, they would have coffee. She added quickly that coffee was probably not on his mind. No, coffee was not on his mind. She opened her handbag and took out the envelope with the MoU. She wanted him to agree that it could now be treated as terminated. He did. There were no grounds for him to disagree. She asked if they might take that long drive again. For old times' sake. They sang, not with gusto, but with a correctness, repeating in exactly the same order the songs they had sung years ago. When they returned they went to her table at the far end.

She allowed him to hold her hands. She spoke first again.

"You have a question to ask."

"Yes, indeed. And you know what it is."

She said she was sure that he would understand. Then, again, she was prepared for him not to understand. He nodded, not knowing why he was going along with this. Should she continue? He nodded again. She stood up, keeping her mug down and shifting the chair in. Was there a problem, he asked?

"Item four."

"Item...?"

"Four. The house rules."

"Ah, yes... of course."

"We will not inflict our pathologies on each other."

"You mean..."

"Just 'some problems' should do."

While he was absorbing this, she started back to her car. He rose, not sure what to do. Should he follow her? Call her back? Fly to her side? She stopped. She turned and watched him. Then she walked back to him and gave him a long, warm hug.

"I have to go now."

She stroked his cheek and walked back to her car. She got in, lowered the window and waved. She drove away.

•••

The Tunnel

They were twins. It was known months before they arrived, of course, but nothing more could be said. The parents abided by the law and did not ask the clinic whether they were boys or girls. Or one boy and one girl. A pigeon pair as such twins are called. When the two girls arrived only the mother caught a glimpse of them before they were sent away to the incubator. The family waiting outside were given the good news and told to return the next day.

The two incubators were marked 011 and 012. The tags mentioned the mother's name below: Vanishree Jayaram. The family and friends gathered around the incubators had the customary expert opinions on all matters pertaining to newborns, especially their acquired appearances. Aunt Matangi's forehead on 011, Ajji's thick mop of hair on 012, the clear differences between the two, and the chalk and cheese distinctions between the noses, as might be expected from the two parental lines. And so on. It was a mere sampler of proclamations wafting down the corridor, keeping the staff at the nursing station amused. They could easily predict them coming. When the duty doctor entered with the practiced greeting the group was emboldened to repeat their observations to her. She listened patiently and then asked Vanishree if the group knew. Vanishree's quiet smile meant she had not had a chance to speak. The duty doctor then informed the group that the girls were identical twins. But the differences...? They would get ironed out within a month, the good doctor explained. In any case, the differences were more imagined than real, she added. Vanishree smiled again. She knew. When she held them at her breasts they were exactly the same. Not in her wildest imagination had she expected to be done with all her childbearing in one stroke.

Since the topic of the evening was imagination the choice of names for the twins was made simple. Kalpana and Bhavana. The one imagined as having Matangi aunty's forehead would be Kalpana. The other, with whatever others had seen in her, was Bhavana. Over the years the imagined differences between Kalpana and Bhavana were indeed eliminated completely. They rolled over on the same day. They crawled, sat up and stood up the same day. They started to scribble on the walls the same day. They giggled together, they howled together, they had tummy runs together. They burrowed into Vanishree's quilt from two sides together. Venu, known in the books as VS Jayaram, the father of the twins, had resigned himself to the loss of Vanishree till the day they would be packed off to a play school.

⁂

It was at play school that the twins blossomed into Kalpana and Bhavana. It happened one morning after the first summer shower. The teacher, keen to get a chat going about rain and where the water comes from, asked the dozen toddlers what they did the previous evening. Silence. Hint hint. What did they see happening outside. Silence. Two hands went up, accompanied by identical grins.

"Yes, Kalpana? Yes, Bhavana?"

What came to be called The KB ping pong duet was born that morning at Kideez Play Garden in RT Nagar. The lines were tossed between Kalpana and Bhavana, completely unrehearsed, as with two jazz musicians playing off each other. It went like this:

"Burrrr! Burrrr!"
"Gajagajagajagaja!"

"Thammathammathammathamma!"
"Dhakadhakadhakadhaka!"
"Water! Thanni! Water!"
"Thanni! Water! Thanni!"
"Jishhh, Jishhh, Jishhh!"
"Phachhak, Phachhak, phachhak!"

The ten other kids had a bellyful. The teacher lost her trained composure momentarily and asked them to shut up. Actually, she only frowned and put her finger to her lips. They shut up quickly anyway. A moment later the teacher laughed too. She looked approvingly at the others, and they joined her. They were now plodding all over the room, ankle deep in the rainwater that had magically covered the floor in a flash.

"Jishhh, Jishhh, Jishhh!"
"Phachhak, Phachhak, phachhak!"

The kids pulled the teacher into the pool. She joined them merrily. She knew the kids had hit a turning point. She also knew deep within that it was not her that did it. It was K and B. Even as she negotiated the swirling waters, laughing, enjoying herself, her sari held up by one hand, the other holding on to a gallant thee-year old lad, she asked K and B how on earth did they think of that. The imagination!

The teacher at Kideez, did not know what the initials RT stood for in RT Nagar. Not surprisingly, most residents of the colony did not know either. There was a bust of a man with long hair and an even longer beard at the junction when you turned off the main road, but you missed it because it was coated with a ten-year supply of dust, packed with exhaust fumes and camouflaged with pigeon droppings. If only they had listened to the old man with the beard the play schools would be so much more fun.

They say that identical twins are formed out of the same soul first, before the organic matter takes shape and is split into an identical pair of bodies. The two souls are said to be connected even if the two bodies are separated by great distances. Dr. Nagaraj, the family physician, who does not believe that there is any such thing as a soul nevertheless accepts that there is something called a mind. And that since the mind is an extension of the brain, it is possible that the minds of identical twins are somehow connected, although not a proven fact by current tenets in neuroscience.

As a matter of fact, when he was explaining this to Vanishree and Venu over tea and bajjis in their home, Bhavana burst into the room, in tears and visibly distressed, and buried herself in Vanishree's lap. Vanishree had learned in four years of child rearing (mother rearing by the girls, she called it) that the first need in any state of emotion is acknowledgement. It applied to all emotions – distress, joy, anger, hurt, anything. A well meant hug before any talk was the rule. Even as she was attending to Bhavana's sobs, the telephone at the other end of the room rang and Venu went to pick it up. It was Veena-akka. It was about Kalpana, who was spending the afternoon at her place. She had slipped and twisted her ankle, and was in great pain. She did not have a car, so could Venu come over and pick up Kalpana? As soon as Venu had made the announcement, and Dr. Nagaraj had offered to go along, Bhavana straightened up, looking so much better.

On the way to Veena-akka's home Bhavana decided to bring some cheer into the car by singing "Row, row, row your boat". Dr. Nagaraj noticed that Vani was singing along softly, her mind still on Kalpana's ankle, praying it was not a fracture or a ripped ligament. When they reached Veena-akka's little bungalow they saw Kalpana in the family's rattan garden sofa, her feet propped up on teapoy with a cushion below them. She was smiling.

Dr. Nagaraj examined her foot, which was now the size and shape of a bharta brinjal, and was sure she must have been in great pain. Veena-akka confessed that she was in a far greater state of distress than Kalpana. Seeing her fret Kalpana had asked her to join in singing songs. They had just sung "Row, row, row your boat" before the car drove in.

Dr. Nagaraj stopped at the Club for a drink and a bite, but lingered far longer at the lounge than usual. He was restless. He reached home late. Mrs. Nagaraj had left instructions on the dining table about clearing up. He showered and changed and switched on the TV. He surfed channels listlessly for a while and switched the set off. He stared at the blank screen, running the after-images in his mind after they had stopped. He moved to his desk, opened the laptop, and entered the key words for his search.

⌘ ⌘ ⌘ ⌘ ⌘

The admission procedure at the primary school of St. Ann's was expected to be long. Vanishree and the girls had decided to make a picnic of it. They had packed sandwiches, bananas and a large flask of orange juice, in addition to bottled water and paper cups. K and B shared games on Vanishree's iPad. After the forms had been submitted, with due verification of documents by Sister Sujata in the office annexe, There was nothing to do but wait. Some mothers continued to stand in the line that went the entire length of the corridor from Class 1, Section A to Class 3, Section D. They stood along the newly painted wall, reminded now and again by a passing nun not to lean against the wall or rest a foot on it. Standing in a line in a school and minding a five-year old at the same time, getting the child with the suddenly found reservoir of energy to behave, anxious that everything is being captured by a hidden camera, is a test of a young mother's fortitude like no other. There were benches under the shade of an old rain tree. Parents were encouraged to wait there till their name was called. It did not work. They preferred to stand in the line, afraid that they might miss the announcement of names.

Vanishree and the girls had their picnic under the tree. They even sang songs. The children in the line were invited to join, but were held back firmly by the mothers. The announcements were heard clearly enough under the tree. "Mrs. Pandit and Jayashree... Mrs. Acharya and Hema...Mrs. Apte and Meenakshi..." Vanishree knew their turn would come much later. If it wasn't for the traffic sounds outside the gate she might have taken a nap on the bench. She pulled out an unread issue of India Today instead.

The girls decided to play a new game they thought up on the way to the school. They opened two new files on the iPad, one for K and one for B. Kalpana began with a line about anything that came to her mind. She could add graphics or a picture taken from any other part of the iPad. She then passed the iPad to B, who had to add a line in the file opened for her. Neither was allowed to see what the other had entered. After they had passed it back and forth with six entries each they would open the two files together and look at the entries as a running text. And laugh. It was Bhavana's turn to start now. They raised it to eight times each. When they had done this four times, raising it to ten times each, they heard their names called: "Mrs. Jayaram and Kalpana and Bhavana..."

When they entered the room they saw a long dining table that could seat twelve. At one end sat the Headmistress, who was known to be Sister Mary Anita. She had two lieutenants, both women, one on either side. One was a nun, clearly from the same order, with a brass badge on her tunic that said Mary Nirmala. All the nuns of this order had the name Mary as a prefix to their names. The other lieutenant appeared to be from the Sikh Regiment. They sat motionless, the lieutenants staring at the entrants and Sister Anita's head buried in the papers before her. Vanishree and the girls waited at the door, not sure if they should enter without being asked. The Headmistress finally made a half-wave gesture, head still down, that seemed to suggest that it was in order to enter, but it did not mean they could sit. Vanishree took two steps forward, hoping that a second command would follow. Or it might be revealed somehow, as in a treasure hunt. K and B had no such hesitation. They marched up swiftly to the end of the table from two sides, halted smartly and pressed their palms together in a firm namaste. The lieutenants looked at Sister Anita, who looked up at last, and after a moment of doubt, returned the Namaste. The two lieutenants followed suit. Sister Anita waved again to suggest that Vanishree could take her seat at the other end of the table while the triumvirate proceeded with the inquisition of the twins.

Sister Anita fired the first salvo.

"Kalpana and Bhavana? Which of you is which?"

"It's simple", said K.

"She's Kalpana", said B.

"And she's Bhavana", said K

"If she is Kalpana, I must be Bhavana", added B.

"Do you both always talk like that? Like a game of ping pong?"

"Not always", said Bhavana.

"Sometimes", added Kalpana.

"Sometimes yes."

"Sometimes no."

Vanishree watched from her assigned seat with some apprehension, not without some delight, as the triumvirate turned their heads to the left, then to the right, as if they were at, well, a ping pong game.

Sister Anita asked what the two of them had been doing under the tree. Yes, she had seen them through the window. The girls explained. Curious, Sister Anita asked if she could see what they had composed. Taking her permission they asked Vanishree at the far end of the table for the iPad. Explaining the entries, passing it between themselves to demonstrate, they showed Sister Anita the end products of two rounds of the game. The first hint of a smile was seen on Sister Anita's face. She looked at the two lieutenants for any comment. They remained expressionless. Sister Anita then asked the girls if they would care to do one for them right there. And could they stand back to back as they did this? Passing the iPad to each other behind their backs? The girls obliged readily. In a minute and a half the two files in the iPad had a new offering. It went like this.

"A cave. I see a cave ahead. Where does it go?".

A set of three concentric circles with the innermost one shaded black.

"Dark and light, day and night".

A set of four circles in a row, blanks and shaded black.

"There is light inside the cave. Off, on, off, on"

A set of four squares one on top of another, blanks and shaded black.

" Zebras are nice, We'll keep two zebras at home."

Two figures of 5, back to back.

"Ducks looking into the cave. They are blocking the entrance."

Eight figures of 2 in a row.

"You can see half a zebra at day time, half at night time."

Four circles, showing a sun and a moon, a sun and a moon.

"Shall we carry on?", asked K.

"Shall we?", asked B.

"No, thank you". Sister Anita seemed to have made up her mind. She looked at the lieutenants. The Sikh Regiment nodded in the north-south axis. Sister Nirmala's head vibrated in the east-west axis. Sister Anita looked at Vanishree at last and asked if she was the mother. On assuring herself that she was, she pronounced the Standard Announcement in Cases of Doubt from the Admissions Manual: "We shall let you know within a few days."

After Vanishree and the girls had left the room Sister Anita addressed her lieutenants, beginning with her own assessment.

"I think we should take them in. But I see that there is some reservation in your minds." Once Sister Anita's verdict was known the Sikh Regiment endorsed it immediately, unqualified. "Yes, yes, yes, we must take them in." It was an exceptionally long sentence, delivered facing forward still.

"And you, sister...?" The neck and face vibrated again. On probing it was revealed that there was a pair of girl twins in her family tree, and they had brought bad luck to the household. Sister Anita listened patiently, making notes about referring her to the counsellor in the convent. When the barrage subsided, Sister Anita asserted that it would be good for the school to have the twins on their rolls. She saw a strategic value to the school from their presence. "Yes, yes, yes, yes" on one side was offset with a knitted brow and eyes shut tight on the other.

"I cannot be held responsible if there is trouble in the school with them here!"

She was finally calmed by two assurances from Sister Anita. First, they would not be in her wing, but in Sister Anita's wing. Second, the girls could be kept apart and put in two separate sections. Relieved and satisfied, Sister Nirmala put her signature on the assessment form, but not without some ceremonious protestations. "No, no, no, no, it's not like that. They can be in my wing. It's all right. It's just that..." Sister Anita thanked her for her thoughtfulness and offered to put one girl in her wing – she could choose which one – and one in her own. Since the two girls looked identical, as they were supposed to, and since they sounded the same too, Sister Nirmala went by the colour of the hair band that Kalpana wore. "The one with the pink hair band", she said. Bhavana went to Sister Anita.

⌘ ⌘ ⌘ ⌘ ⌘

K and B did not seem to mind the separation at all. They had enough time with each other at home and on holidays. They made new friends in their sections and some even got to be common friends. The real difference was of another kind. If Sister Anita was content with her admission decision Sister Nirmala was determined to prove her wrong. It should not be difficult to imagine how something like that works. Educationists call it by different names – the self-fulfilling prophecy, the Pygmallion effect, and so on. It was not without its comic moments. Every now and then Sister Nirmala would confront Bhavana in the corridor or in the dining hall and admonish her for a lapse like "Look where you are going", or "Learn to behave yourself", or "Can't you do anything right?". B would smile and point to the name tag on her pinafore.

And it was not uncommon for Sister Anita to tell Kalpana that she was doing fine in class, and that she should keep it up. Kalpana, too, would smile, knowing the compliment was really meant for Bhavana.

There was one kind of separation that was a different experience. It was called detention. The first time Sister Nirmala used it was when Kalpana answered questions in English Grammar class. She had been asked the plural of fish and had replied that it was fish, but that it could sometimes be fishes. That was not the answer Sister Nirmala wanted. To put Kalpana in her place she asked, not without some derision, what else she knew about fish that the class might not know. K replied that a famous English writer called George Bernard Shaw had spelt fish differently. It was G-H-O-T-I.

"Being over smart, eh?" She did not say anything more at that time, but the children knew her mind was working on something sinister through the rest of the class. When the bell rang and the children stood up for permission to leave the room, Sister Nirmala made the announcement. "You may leave. Kalpana Jayaram will stay back." When Vani came by to pick up the girls she was told about the detention. Not the least inclined to question Sister Nirmala or the school about the punishment she decided to drop Bhavana home and return for Kalpana later. Sister Nirmala was disappointed that Kalpana's mother had not confronted her.

There were two more detentions through the year. The last one was on a Friday just before the vacation. Bhavana had an essay to submit at Venu's Lions Club Children's festival, so she hurried back. Vani would send a driver to fetch Kalpana when the school telephoned. The office was given the driver's mobile phone number. He would take Kalpana directly to the Lion's Club.

Bhavana had decided to write about the family's train ride from Pune to Mumbai. It was the most joyous experience ever in the Jayaram family. And the high point of the train ride was the tunnel! It was the first time the girls had ever ridden through a tunnel. And there were twenty eight of them! The family played their own version of antakshari through the ghat section. Each time the train entered a tunnel one of the girls would sing two to four lines of a song that was completely made up. Vani and Venu would repeat the lines. On their last note the other girl had to continue the song filling in her own two to four lines. At first the others in the carriage looked on with curiosity. Very soon they had all converged on the family, joining Vani and Venu with the fillers and waiting to hear what the girls were cooking up. It was a delightfully mad chop suey of words, phrases, figures of speech, sounds, images, nonsense words and nonsense rhymes.

Bhavana sat at the place marked for her. She took out the two pencils, eraser and pencil sharpener from the pouch and placed them at the ready. The sheets of A-4 size paper were distributed, three sheets per child. A bell was rung to signal the start. Bhavana closed her eyes for a few moments and calmed her breathing, a practice she had acquired from her mother.

The images started to appear, but not as expected. It began with the jumble of voices in the dark, overlayed with the sound of giant wheels thundering on the track. When the light appeared Bhavana saw that the train was pulling backwards, leaving the tunnel in front. The family and all the others in the carriage shouted together, "STOP!" In deference to their wishes the train slowed down and groaned to a stop. The passengers looked at each other. They realized in an instant that they had some power over the train. In perfect unison they now shouted, "FORWARD!", and turned towards the tunnel to watch the train go through again. The train did not move. From the tunnel came the sound of another train. It rushed out, hurtling forward at their own train, growing larger by the split second. Kalpana opened the antakshari with a "No!" A chorus of voices followed with "No, no, no, no, no!" Bhavana followed it up with "Go!"All passengers in all carriages could now be heard chanting "Go, go, go, go, go!"The train in front exploded like a length of Diwali Red Fort crackers, and turned into a huge cloud of soap bubbles. Tiny bubbles, large bubbles, bubbles the size of peas, marbles, tennis balls and basket balls. The bubbles were now floating past their train. They floated above the train, below, to the right and left and even through the insides of the carriages. They reflected many colours from the evening sun. They reflected the faces of passengers, every bubble with a face sealed within it. Four of the bubbles hovered in front of Bhavana and parked themselves there. Every one of them had Kalpana's face, the way she always looked calling Bhavana out to play.

Bhavana opened her eyes. She remembered her mother's advice to always write whatever came to her mind, and to never think about making it look good. Bhavana picked up her pencil, held it against the sheet of paper for a whole minute, put back her things in the pouch and left the room. She stepped outside and saw Vani seated on the verandah reading a magazine. Avoiding her carefully Bhavana went to the lawn and sat on a swing. Realizing that it was very unusual, Vani went up to her and sat on the next swing. They sat on the swings without saying a word, the feet just about in contact with the grass below, moving hardly a foot in either direction.

The car at last. It drove in through the Club gate at a faster than usual speed. Mother and daughter left the swings and walked briskly to the car. Sister Anita was in the car. And there was no sign of Kalpana. Sister Anita got out of the car, apologizing profusely and begging them to get into the car quickly. She would accompany them personally to St. Martha's Hospital where the school doctor had taken Kalpana.

On the way to the hospital Sister Anita explained what had happened. She was apologizing again. Sister Nirmala, in her determination to make a mark on Kalpana, had locked her in the classroom before going to the staff room for her evening tea. Kalpana had started to protest and cry, saying she had done no wrong, and that she had to be with her sister for something important that evening. Sister Nirmala decided to discipline Kalpana further and locked her in the closet where the class stored stationery, play material and games equipment. After tea there was a staff meeting to discuss vacation duties and she went there directly.

When the driver did not receive a call from the school he decided to go there anyway. He saw that the classroom was empty. He went to the Headmistress' office to enquire. That is how Sister Anita came to know about the accident. Kalpana had passed out in the closet. She had suffered a concussion on falling and there was a cardiac dysrhythmia that had not been explained fully yet. She was in an ICU at St. Martha's. The hospital staff had said she was out of danger, although it was a serious episode for one so small.

On reaching the ICU they saw that Kalpana was sleeping, but appeared restless. The nurse said she was delirious a while ago. She had calmed down now, but her breathing was still erratic. Only one person was allowed to go in at a time. Vani looked at Bhavana and signaled to her to enter. She did, moving quietly to her side near her head. Bhavana bent to look her sister in the face, gazing into a mirror. She was calm now, slipping into deep sleep. When she straightened up she saw Kalpana offering her hand. Bhavana took it in her own and sat on the stool next to the bed. There were two tear drops below Kalpana's eyes. Bhavana wiped them gently, only to find two tears welling up in her own eyes. There was now a smile on Kalpana's face. Bhavana could now leave and send her mother in.

[Do identical twins really have telepathic abilities? Is there any scientific evidence? What seems to make the difference is exactly when the division of the zygote (fertilized egg) takes place. This can take place almost immediately, or up to twelve days later. What is seen is that 'late splitters' develop extremely close bonds after birth, bonds that can last a lifetime, whereas 'early splitters' become more independent, and regard each other just like an ordinary brother or sister. Sure enough, when experiments were carried out in London and Copenhagen, on each occasion it was a late-splitting pair who showed the clearest evidence for telepathy on their polygraph charts. The often heard critical complaint that there is no repeatable experiment for any kind of psychic effect appears no longer true.]

The Visitor

It was his first visit to a Police Station. He had never imagined he would be stepping into one on his sixtieth birthday. He did not know what to expect. Police Station scenes in the movies had extras with paunches playing the parts of policemen, the caps fitted carelessly over heads that badly needed haircuts. The policemen were always dark, with oily skin. On one side there was usually a lockup that had a steel door with bars. Behind the bars there was either a vicious looking bearded man in a vest and lungi or a man seated in a corner with a ghostly stare.

The Police Station in SP Nagar was in a middle class residential area. People walking past the high brick and mortar walls generally avoided looking in when they passed the gate. They walked just a wee bit faster. When he stepped inside from the road he saw three rows of flower beds on either side of the path leading to the arched entrance. The front was all granite, rather like a fort, with two windows on the left and two on the right. The windows had arches to match the entrance, the outline of stones standing out an inch from the wall. Looking up, he saw a sculpture at the top. It had two elephants standing on their hind legs, they seemed to be wrestling. Just below that was a black stone slab embedded in the wall with the year of the building's inauguration. The silver aluminium paint in the grooves read 1905. A voice from within the entrance greeted him in Kannada.

"Namaskara. Please come in. What can I do for you?"

He stepped into the reception area and saw that it was a policeman on duty, standing at ease with a standard Enfield World War II carbine on his right side, held at an angle away from his straight frame. He had no paunch. The cap was fitted straight on a head that had a smart haircut. He was standing erect. He was smiling.

"What can I do for you?" he asked once again.

"I came to report..." he began hesitatingly in English.

"FIR? Please take a seat at the bench. SHO saheb will be here soon." The constable nodded his head in the direction of a bench and a table. The visitor mumbled a thanks and stepped towards the bench.

"Don't know Kannada?" Before he could answer, the constable added in local Dakhani-Urdu that it was no problem. There were lots of non-Kannadigas in SP Nagar, and the Station handled cases in English as well. The visitor took his seat. The constable added that Station House Officer himself was from a Goan family.

"Where in SP Nagar?"

"Eighth Main".

"Near lawyer Swamy's house?"

"Yes". He tried to keep the conversation to the bare minimum.

"After the transformer of before?"

"In between."

"Aah, the house with the green gate! I have seen you on Eighth Main."

"Yes, green gate."

"You have a little white dog in the compound. Keeps barking at people passing the gate. Kav kav kav kav! He barks and turns in a circle, barks again, turns again!"

"Yes, that's the house". I am sorry if the dog..."

"No, no, nothing like that. I am not complaining. I like the little fellow. I sometimes bark back at him. Kav kav kav. He keeps quiet then."

"He is harmless, really. He doesn't bite. Only barks."

"Good, no? Dogs must bark. That is their job. What is the point in keeping a dog if it does not bark?"

"The SHO, is he...? Should I come later?"

"Any minute, any minute. He is taking a call inside. Is it urgent? Shall I call another officer from inside?"

"No, not urgent."

"Not urgent, but important. Of course!"

"I will wait."

Just then there was the sound of approaching footsteps that only Oxford patent leather shoes can produce. It had to be the SHO. The constable nodded in the direction of the passage to let him know that the wait had ended.

"Inspector DeSouza sir. I told you he would be here soon."

The Inspector walked in briskly, extended his hand, asked the visitor to remain seated, and took his place on the other side of the table. The policeman briefed the Inspector for the meeting.

"FIR, sir. Eighth Main house. Green gate, dog. Maharashtrian family. Doesn't know Kannada. Hindi-English."

The Inspector began to explain the procedure as he took out a register, sheets of blank paper, a pair of rubber stamps and a stamp pad from a drawer. He assured him that he could report the case in either English or Hindi. It would be recorded in Kannada, and translated to him in English before it was filed.

The Inspector then asked him if he was carrying any photo ID and proof of residence, explaining that these could be produced even after the FIR was recorded.

The visitor took out his Driving License and the Inspector confirmed that it would serve the purpose. He began straight away, opening the register to a fresh page and entering the date and time at the top right hand corner. The visitor found himself drawn into the Inspector's rapidly posed questions.

Name...Father's name...Age...Address...Phone numbers... Number of persons residing at address...Relationships...He stopped. The preliminaries done, he looked up and asked the visitor to narrate the case.

"Hmmm. Mr. Vinayak Hari Kulkarni, 23-B Eighth Main. Where have I seen you before? No matter, tell me about the case now."

There was no response from the visitor.

"At a loss for words? It happens. You must have gone through this several times in your mind before coming here. Everybody does that. But when the time comes we can't find the words to say!" The Inspector laughed gently.

The visitor looked at the Inspector, then at the window on the right, then at the constable on the left, standing at ease. The constable nodded his head in the direction of the Inspector encouragingly. Seeing him hesitating, the Inspector asked if he could order a cup of tea. The visitor shook his head as politely as he could to decline. The Inspector changed to a more comforting tone, assuring him that he should feel completely free to say anything that was in his mind, and that the final entry in the FIR would be only after he had his confirmation of the statement.

Even as the visitor was recalling the scene of the Police Station in the last Hindi movie, the Inspector added, "It is not like the silly bloody scenes they show in films. We are here to serve society, to serve you."

The visitor looked once more at the policeman standing at ease, who nodded in the direction of the Inspector once again and smiled. He cleared his throat and began.

"There has been a death..."

"Aah, now we are getting somewhere", said the SHO. "Yes, tell me about it."

"It was ten days ago."

"Not known till now? Not reported?"

"It is known. It was in the newspapers."

By now the Inspector had reached into the drawer and switched on the voice recorder with a practiced hand. Something told him this case was different, it was going to be important.

"What do you wish to tell me about the death? Whose death are you referring to?"

"Vinayak Hari Kulkarni."

"That is..." The Inspector looked down at the register and then at the visitor again. "That is your name, is it not?"

"Yes. That was my name. I died ten days ago."

"Come, sir! This is not the place for...Filing an FIR is a serious matter."

"The eleventh day ceremony is tomorrow. It will be at the choultry next to the Ganesha temple. Please come. This is a personal invitation." Turning to the constable, he repeated, "You too. Please come."

The Inspector decided to go along with it for a while. He asked at what time they should be at the choultry, if it was all right to come in uniform, as he may be on duty, and if he, Vinayak Hari Kulkarni, would be there himself to receive him. The visitor replied in a tone that echoed the Inspector.

"Come, sir! This is not the time for...The eleventh day ceremony is a serious matter."

"So is filing an FIR", replied the Inspector, his voice turning a bit stern now. "Are you or are you not here to file an FIR?"

"Yes, that is what I am here for."

"Then let us get down to the job. Enough of the joking. What is the case?"

"A death."

"A death", repeated the Inspector, half suspecting the visitor had not grasped the point made a moment ago. "You are reporting a death."

"A death ten days ago, and the eleventh day ceremony is tomorrow."

The Inspector glanced at the policeman on duty, who responded by tapping his temple with the forefinger of his free hand. With another nod of his head he was asking if he should eject the intruder from the premises. The Inspector decided to keep his cool and take on the visitor. There was no urgent case demanding attention that morning. He could have some fun. Who knows, it might turn out an interesting morning.

"An eleventh day ceremony is not a subject for an FIR."

"Is there a list of subjects that qualify for an FIR?"

"Yes, there is."

"Is there a list of subjects that are not permitted in an FIR?"

"That which is not in the list of permitted subjects is not permitted. An eleventh day ceremony is not a subject for an FIR." The Inspector had clearly scored a point. He allowed himself a grin with flared nostrils. The visitor nodded to acknowledge the point made, but his knitted brow said he was not convinced.

"The eleventh day ceremony can only be after a death ten days earlier. A death is accepted as a subject for an FIR?"

"Yes, when reported by one who is not himself the deceased."

"Is there a law that a death may not be reported by the person who has died?"

The Inspector was now compelled to look the visitor in the eye and give him the stare he had been taught at the Police Academy. It was the one to be used in interrogations that says we have you now, and you better come out straight. It had to be given from a distance of eight inches from the face and directed at a point between the two eyes, accompanied by a state that is called a penetrating silence.

The visitor rephrased his question, "Non-permissible list?"

It did not work. The Inspector really had no precedence to fall back upon, so he did what was best under the condition. He rose and called the meeting to a close by suggesting to Mr. Vinayak Hari Kulkarni that he go home, think about the matter with a cool head. He was welcome to return to the Station after he had thought about it some more. He even gave the visitor two phone numbers on a slip of paper and suggested that he call before dropping in. He then pointed to the arched entrance.

The visitor rose and left the Inspector's table. He moved quickly in the opposite direction, through the corridor into the next room with the lock-up. He entered it unhesitatingly and closed the steel door with the bars. Clang.

⁂

The policeman on duty tapped his temple with the forefinger of his free hand once again. The SHO was not amused. He ordered the constable to get the visitor out of the lock up and send him out.

"Forcibly?" asked the policeman.

"Of course!"

"By the collar?" The constable was aware of recent media splashes about police conduct. They had used words like excesses and atrocities. The constable was a nice man, after all. He found violence of any kind distasteful. Just the other day the owner of the kirana shop had shown him a Kannada newspaper with a photo of a police party dispersing a mob and asked him jokingly what atrocities he had planned for the day. The hangers on had laughed. The constable laughed too. They were good natured jokes from nice people of the neighbourhood. They knew the constable was a nice guy. He would never use force unless ordered by a superior.

"If necessary, yes, by the collar", confirmed the Inspector. It was an order.

The policeman rested his carbine on the stand, picked up a baton, looked at the SHO once again and went inside to the lockup. The Inspector began to tap the table with his knuckles, waiting for the reappearance of the constable, the visitor in tow. He heard the sound of the lockup door open. Clang.

"Kav kav - kav kav!" It was the bark of a small dog. It was followed by the voice of the constable, barking back, "Kav - kav kav!"

Just as the Inspector rose to go to the lockup himself the constable entered with a small Pomeranian, held up high by the collar. The dog was barking away in protest, "Kav kav - kav kav!" The policeman was barking back, half lovingly, "Kav - kav kav!"

"I will leave him home", said the constable, as he left the Station and turned towards Eighth Main. The sound of the dog barking and the policeman's rejoinders started to fade away. The Inspector rushed to the gate and called after the constable.

"Find out more about Vinayak Hari Kulkarni when you get there!"

⌘ ⌘ ⌘ ⌘ ⌘

Inspector DeSouza was about to resume his seat when he thought it would be correct if he went inside and looked into the lockup himself. To be on the safe side he checked if his .38 caliber service pistol was loaded. Putting it back into its holster he proceeded towards the lockup inside. It was indeed empty. He picked up the hailer from above the filing cabinet and flicked on the switch. Blocking the corridor leading to the front he barked his orders in the direction of the rooms inside.

"Mr. Vinayak Hari Kulkarni! This is Inspector DeSouza. Please report to me immediately. Your unauthorized presence inside the police station is an offence. I am giving you exactly 30 seconds to come out and present yourself before me. After that I will be forced to take any action that may be necessary to have you arrested!"

Hearing the Inspector's booming voice all the policemen in the Station rushed to the corridor from all the rooms. They ranged in rank from probationers to a Havildar. They stared at the Inspector in bewilderment. What was on? Was it too much drink? They had seen Inspector DeSouza in rage before, but never in a wild eyed state like this. By now he had taken his service pistol out and was waving it about as he commanded the men.

"Search every corner of every room! He must be in there somewhere! There is no way out from the back. I am guarding the entrance, so he cannot escape from the front! Go! Don't stand there staring at me! Go and find him!"

"Go and get who, sir?" asked the Havildar.

"Him! That Vinayak Hari Kulkarni!"

Scramble! They found no one. They looked behind every steel almirah and under every table and camp cot. The armoury was unlocked and relocked three times under the joint supervision of the Havildar and the Sub-inspector. They crawled into the dog kennel and climbed into the water tank above. Mr. Vinayak Hari Kulkarni was nowhere in the premises of the SP Nagar Police Station.

Inspector DeSouza sat down to make an entry in the log book, a duty he could not avoid as all the men in the Station had been mobilized for an encounter. A replacement policeman on duty watched through the corner of his eye as the Inspector began to write. The Station telephone rang. The Inspector picked up the phone. The voice at the other end was polite.

"Please do come for the eleventh day ceremony. Please stay for lunch." Click.

The Inspector saw that the constable was watching. He put the receiver down with a bang, cursing "Bloody wrong numbers! On the bloody increase!"

The policeman who had taken the dog out returned. He had the smile that said he had found out something important. The inspector asked him to sit at the bench and report his findings.

"The pooja was just over. They were serving prasad. Very nice shira."

"Yes, yes. What about that Vinayak Hari fellow?"

The constable sat still for a few moments, looking straight ahead past the inspector. He cleared his throat and began.

"There has been a death..."

"Aah, now we are getting somewhere", said the SHO. "Yes, tell me about it."

"It was ten days ago."

"What did you find out about the death? Whose death are you referring to?"

"Vinayak Hari Kulkarni. He died just before he turned sixty."

"That is... The person who was here an hour ago?"

"Yes. That was my name. I died ten days ago."

The Writ

It was his turn. He did not hesitate a moment to choose. He took the set of three pens. They were displayed in the open leather-bound case. The name Waterman was engraved in gold on the case. There were three identical pens. You had to look closely to see the embedded dot above the silver rim of the cap. The dots were black, red and green to show the ink in the pen. Papa wrote with all the three pens, knowing what things needed which colour. Entries in account books were always in green. There was one account book for each year for the last thirty years.

The youngest of four children, Anmol was not expected to be vocal about choices. He had grown up allowing others to speak first. He really longed to possess the pens. He was overjoyed that the others had let him take them. He did not reveal his joy, of course. He was not expected to be more expressive than necessary. The others were Anant, the oldest, and the sisters Anahita and Aparajita. They had gone their ways long ago. Anant had a job in Mumbai, which demanded frequent travel to Singapore. Anahita had married and moved to Delhi. Aparajita was in college studying for an M.Phil. in History. She had shifted to an apartment with two other girls after tiring of the rubbery rotis in the hostel. Anmol was the youngest. He was happy with the Management Trainee appointment in a Private Sector Bank. He chose to stay back in Hyderabad and look after Amma. Together they also looked after Dadiji staying in the same house. They were on the first floor of a two-storeyed duplex. The family had gathered for the first Diwali after Papa's departure. It was the time to look into Papa's belongings and decide what to do with them.

The pens were part of a kit. It included a large board with the corners capped with leather triangles. This permitted easy change of sheets to cover the board. The board was kept on a small desk of rosewood with two drawers. The seashell shaped handles of the drawers were shiny brass. The far end of the desk had two receptacles for inkwells. The inkwells were not in use, but were in place in the desk. There was a half-moon blotting pad. A brown paper cover had a collection of blotting paper sheets for the pad, cut to the right size for quick replacement. There was a wooden ruler. The children always called it a roller. Papa corrected them to say it was a ruler, showing them how it should be used. There was a decorative Moradabad brass bowl with three compartments to hold needle pins, drawing pins and paper clips. There were the pens. Amma thought that any one of them should take the entire set, table and all. The children did not choose any of the other things. Anmol gat the entire set. Amma was pleased. It would remain in the house.

Papa's clothes, especially his collection of suits and ties, were given away to a charity. Anant and Anmol kept one tie each. Anahita chose one coat to take back for her husband. Aparajita left the room, wiping her tears. The family also gifted the steel almirah to the charity. The eight pairs of shoes were taken by the family mochi.

Two days after Diwali the house was quiet again. Dadi asked Anmol to sit with her as they watched old movies. Amma chose Dev Anand hits.

⌘ ⌘ ⌘ ⌘ ⌘

It was past midnight. Dadi and Amma had retired. Anmol found himself not one bit sleepy. He tried to read. He listened to some music on his earphones. He thought he would try out the pens. He decided to write an essay on Papa looking down on the family as they remembered him with a room full of his belongings. Yes, he would write when things were still fresh in his mind.

He sat at Papa's desk and opened a fresh writing pad. He took out the pen with the blue dot, opened the cap and put pen to paper. He had already thought of the opening line. It would be: Papa joined us today. He had barely placed the shiny gold plated nib on the pad when he felt it move by itself. The title appeared before him at the top of the page. It was in Hindi, in capital letters: DEKHA SUNA NA KAAN. The nib moved again, this time to the left margin, and wrote the first line. This time it was in English: Papa joined us today.

Anmol lifted the pen off the pad and capped it quickly. He sat still, gazing at the page before him with a title and a first line. He closed his eyes. He saw lines appearing on the pad, the page filling up, the pages turned, and more writing on the pages opened. He could not tell what was written, but it was a neat handwriting. He felt his writing hand being tugged. He held it back with his free hand. Putting down the pen he covered his eyes with both palms and leaned back. A voice appeared, humming notes, distant, faint, but clear. Very slowly and methodically it was repeating a cycle of notes, hummed gently. He recognized the notes... re...ni...dha...ma...ga...re... sa. It was elegiac, as expected, bound in sorrow, but it had an enveloping quality to it. Anmol wanted the volume increased, but it stayed soft and distant. It did not matter. Anmol was now bathed in a tranquil raga, defying grief. His breath eased, breathing in, pausing, breathing out, pausing longer, sailing gently with the notes in the distance.

The first barks on the street below were always from the black Labrador, urging his master to hurry out of the front door. This was followed by the complaining yelps of two strays who did not think the day had yet begun. Anmol awoke when a scooter drove past and all three dogs turned their barks on the rider. It was half past five. He put the pen back in its case. When he turned to the pad he saw that writing on three pages had disappeared. Only the title and the first line remained. In Hindi and English. The handwriting was his. He was tempted greatly to open the pen and write a few more lines about his father watching over the family gathering.

He put the thought aside and decided to try out the second pen, the one with the green ink. He took out a sheet of A-4 paper from the pack kept next to the desktop printer and placed it on the board. He took out the pen with the green dot. He would write a short poem, just a couplet perhaps, the one from Kabirdas on dekha suna na kaan. The nib moved. It entered the expenses of the previous day...the rickshaw-walla, the delivery boy for snacks...Anmol watched in fascination as the nib continued. The tip for the gas cylinder exchange, the two bars of Lux toilet soap, packet of kishmish, the dhobi, the wandering mystic with his one-stringed gourd... Four columns. Serial number, item, quantity, amount. All in green.

He knew he had to start on the morning chores in the kitchen. He tidied up the desk and put the pen back. He was curious. What would the pen with the black ink do? The kitchen jobs could wait a bit. This time he opened a diary in which his last entry was over a year ago. He put aside the cap with the black dot, looked at the nib with a smile and asked it gently what it had in store for him. The pen wagged and moved his hand to the diary. The ruled opened page was blank. The first line appeared as soon as the nib touched the page…

re...ni...dha...ma...ga...re...sa

Leaving a line, the writing continued below. It was a letter in verse. The writing was centred on the page, the lines of different lengths forming a symmetrical pattern.

For my beloved Anjana
As the dawn prepares to break
It is the time for sweet dreams
As you dream your sweetest dream
You know not how much I love you.
I loved you the first time I saw you
I loved you the first time you looked
In my direction, smiling
I knew I loved you then.
I know I love you still
I love you when you frown
I love you when you stare ahead
Not looking at me.
Not looking at anybody
Not looking at anything
I love you not looking at me
I love you still.

It was done. Anmol had struggled for weeks to find words for a letter to Anjana. Not seeing any response from her, he wanted to let her know of his agony through a letter. Speaking to her was not the same thing, and he did not have what it took to confront her. It had to be a letter. His prose was not working. He had torn up many notes. And now...it was done.

⌘ ⌘ ⌘ ⌘ ⌘

At the office Anmol was making a presentation that was going to decide his future. The company wanted him to go into investment management. His heart was in marketing. He had put together a set of eighteen slides accompanied by video clips and an electronic audio track. He rehearsed it many times, adding, subtracting, prettifying, until it looked perfect. He argued that the Company should steadily grow an image for itself as being in the Nation Building business. It worked. The senior managers wondered where he had been hiding all this time. He got the marketing job. He had worn a jacket for the occasion. The three pens adorned his lapel pocket. On his way out the GM patted Anmol and said that he envied his collection of pens.

On his way home he picked up a box of Amma's favourite combo of kachori and jalebi. Before he could break the news she announced that there was a letter for him delivered by a driver. It was kept on the dining table. He gave her a big hug, pressed the box in her hands and said he would bring a plate from the kitchen. They had to be eaten hot. He passed the dining table, stopped, and looked at the envelope. It was Anjana's handwriting. He picked up the plate and stopped at the table again. His fingers trembled as he opened the top of the envelope, half inch by half inch. The stationery was handmade, lavender, with tiny petals embedded in the paper. It was perfumed. It was folded twice along the width, the outer side blank. When he opened the sheet he caught the opening lines.

My dearest...

Anmol sat down and pressed the page to his chest. Amma called from the living room. Was he getting the plate or what. Anmol got a snapshot view of the rest of the page. There were four lines. He picked up the plate and rushed out. Amma asked if he had seen the letter on the table. No, he hadn't – sorry, yes, he had – but he hadn't read it yet. He would read it in his room later. Amma asked him to go back and read it. She would have the kachori and jalebi. Obedient Anmol went back inside. He opened the letter again, sitting down on a chair. The four lines were spaced neatly in the middle of the page.

I cannot write the way you do.

Meeting would be so much nicer.

Longing to know when.

Yours in truth.

He put the letter back into the cover, tucked it into his shirt pocket and hurried back to Amma. She saw the envelope sticking out and asked if it was something important. Anmol nodded. Something special? Anmol avoided her gaze and mumbled, maybe. She patted the place next to her on the sofa and made him sit. "It is from Anjana, is it not?" Anmol looked up and was looking for words, when she added, "Papa liked her. Call her home some time."

[It is said that when the legendary musician Miyan Tansen passed away his son Bilas Khan was expected to sing at the funeral. He chose to sing in Todi Raga, usually associated with grief and somber occasions. As he started, the notes took an altered scale by themselves. He continued with the scale and completed his rendition. It came to be called Bilaskhani Todi later on.]

About the Author

Vijay Padaki is a Theatre Educator based in Bangalore. He has worn many caps all his life with equal facility. Among them, he has been active in the theatre for over sixty years. He has been a management professional for over forty-five years.

Vijay joined Bangalore Little Theatre in 1960, the year of its inception, and later served the company in many capacities – as actor, director, trainer, writer, designer and administrator. In 2008, Bangalore Little Theatre Foundation was restructured as a Public Charitable Trust. It was done with the purpose of reinforcing the organisation's commitment to social development goals beyond performance. The Trust requested Vijay to provide the leadership to a newly-created Academy of Theatre Arts in its formative years.

Vijay has been responsible for institutionalizing several activities of BLT, such as the annual summer workshop for newcomers to the theatre (SPOT), from which has emerged a large number of the theatre personalities in Bangalore, the History of Ideas programme of biographical plays, the Courtyard Theatre programme, and the Children's Theatre programme, which includes the annual flagship children's play as a partnership production to support a charity. Vijay conceived and initiated programmes for training trainers, training directors and promoting new writing for the stage. He has forged several international partnerships with BLT over the years. The Ministry of Culture invited Vijay to initiate a programme of Arts and Heritage Management in India.

Vijay has been a writer for many years. In addition to over 50 original plays published by Bangalore Little Theatre, he diversified into writing short stories. There are over 40 stories by him. He has done several readings of his stories in public spaces. Notion is publishing the first 36 stories in two volumes. Vijay believes that all writing is autobiographical. (To greater or lesser extent!) What that means is that life experiences have a way of creeping into everything we say. In other words, there is no need to deny it or be sorry about it. He says he has had the good fortune of exposures in life that had both breadth and depth. These included field experiences as part of his work in large development programmes in rural settings.

Vijay is a psychologist and behavioural scientist by training, and founder-director of a management resource centre with programmes of research, consulting and training in the areas of Organisation and Institutional Development. A good part of his work was devoted to the effectiveness of large development programmes. Among his earlier assignments he was a member of the founding faculty at Indian Institute of Management, Bangalore, the founder of a Centre for Management for the textile industry in Ahmedabad, and a Visiting Professor at Indian Institute of Science, Bangalore. He was a Senior Associate at the National Institute of Advanced Studies in its early years.

www.ingramcontent.com/pod-product-compliance
Lightning Source LLC
LaVergne TN
LVHW091306150826
845673LV00006B/1557

9798895886595